LIFE IN A NUTSHELL

By Karen Parsonson

Table of Contents

Chapter 1: Ending and Beginning

I can't believe it's come to this: here I am at a fancy jazz bar, all dressed up to go to a rock 'n roll bar. My girl-friend/ex-assistant and best friend Alixe had bugged me to get out after almost 20 years out of the dating game. Who was I kidding? At 42 years old, my (hopefully) soon-to-be ex- had done the unthinkable - had an affair with a client and I was the last to know. They were probably blissfully happy enjoying stolen moments together and here I was, being slobbered over by some guy blubbering about his life to me while Alixe waltzed around the dance-floor from partner to partner.

The place was cool enough: all decked-out in shades of blue, full of lots of 30-plus-somethings looking hopefully for Mr. or Ms.-Right-for-the-Night, but I just wanted to be back home, the past 5 months erased forever, making pizza with the kids on a Saturday night. Startled out of my reverie while politely nodding absentmindedly to the guy with the sob-story, I heard a warm, masculine voice politely ask me to dance. Turning, the proverbial (was it even possible?) tall-dark-handsome stranger held out his hand invitingly. Something about the sparkle in his eyes and the sincerity in his voice told me it was alright.

I nervously explained that I had never danced to jazz music before

4

and was more of a die-hard (albeit old-in-the-tooth) head-banger, but he smiled warmly at me and said we'd "take it slow". Who was I to refuse? So, leaving the sad guy (who was still talking, now really to himself) at the table, I slowly followed in the wake of the stranger who directed me gently through the masses to the dance-floor.

Now understand...I took ballet for 10 years as a kid and teen but have never been able to "follow" or let a partner on the dance floor "take the lead". Once, I had signed the ex- (he-who-shall-not-be-named, Jeff) up for ballroom dance classes with me - something to do together. The kids <u>loved</u> to see us dressed up for practice nights. Our teacher would always bemoan to me (as he took each of the women from the couples up to demonstrate steps) to "give up control!", but even just hearing that grated me to the core. I wasn't a great giver-up-controller...

So here I am, face-to-face with Mr. TDH (Tall Dark & Handsome), who is named Tony and he is gracefully escorting me around the dance-floor. Are we actually dancing or am I floating and watching all of this? Alixe trots past me on the dance-floor, grins and winks, giving me a thumbs-up like I'm back in high-school at the prom. Tony expertly glides us along, smiling and somehow maneuvering me where I'm supposed to go. I don't even notice anyone else is on the dance-floor at all! I'm totally enjoying this, and he makes it seem so easy. The panic gone, I notice his warm, masculine smell, the timbre of his voice, his dark brown eyes twinkling in merriment, his shining black hair coiffed so perfectly, the smooth muscles of his arms and back - it had been a long time since I'd felt like an appealing woman in another man's arms...

The song finished, and Tony walked me back to the table, then out for a smoke - yes, I am in that wretched, detested minority of people who will not be guilted/terrified/bullied/inconvenienced into quitting. And so was Tony. Amazingly, we both smoked the same brand of Benson & Hedges 100's - although mine were menthol - "tic-tacs", as he called them, trying one to see what it was like. Turns out the guy at the table with the sad story was his friend but he (jokingly) denied inflicting him on me to be saved by the handsome prince. We made some polite chatter (he was single, had his own business - a shrink, no-less) and explained that he came from a big family.

My story was more complicated, and I explained simply that I was in the process of a messy divorce, had 2 early-teen kids and a business with my ex-. I guess I figured from the outset that if I was going to scare anyone off, I may as well do it at the beginning. What was there to candy-coat? It is what it is (Alixe's favorite saying), and I had nothing to be ashamed of.

We returned to the dance-floor for the rest of the night. He hadn't run away screaming? I hadn't terrified him with my blunt honesty?

Alright, I had bolstered my courage to even go out for a few coolers, but who I am is who I am. I've never been able to put on a face and present myself any other way, other than in professional situations. My (few) friends who remained after the separation (it was pathetically true that couple friends melted away when the going got tough and they were faced with having a soon-to-be-divorcee in their lives) always told me I wore my heart on my sleeve and couldn't play poker worth a damn. Well, I'd laid out my hand and we'd see how it played out.

The night wore on and I just relaxed and enjoyed myself in Tony's arms on the dance-floor. We went outside for smoke breaks and seemed to talk so comfortably. Alixe was nowhere to be seen - wait a minute, wasn't that her off with a guy in the corner snuggling? But I didn't care. I was enjoying feeling like a woman for the first time in many, many years.

Lights on at the end of the night, the time had come for everyone to see everything and everyone without the soft shadows of romantic lighting. I was set to figure out how to drive Alixe and me back to her place for a sleep-over when Tony suggested he drive us. I was in no shape to drive (too many coolers) and she was with someone else to drive her home. Despite my protest at being fully capable of getting myself to her place (which part of the city did she live in again?), Tony ushered me to his car and we left mine safely parked behind the club.

Believe me, in my right mind I would never even think of letting a stranger I had just met that evening drive me to my friend's house, but he was right - I was in no shape to drive. When we got there, Alixe and what's-his-name were already there and asked Tony in for a drink. We watched music videos on TV, the 4 of us, until things got heated with those two and they excused themselves to go upstairs.

This was it - his chance to run or get my number to "call me sometime", but Tony and I kept on talking. I told him about my crazy, little mixed-up family and life and he told me about his crazy big mixed-up family and his life. We talked about politics (I am a die-hard NDP, he is a Conservative-to-the-bone), religion (he is a Roman Catholic and I am undecided, raised with no religion), relationships and marriage (remember, I'm in a messy divorce after a long and unhappy marriage? - and - he's never been married but had been in a 5-year long-term relationship a few years back, lots of other short-term ones), and our ages. For heaven's sakes, he's 29 and I'm 42 (although he insists I don't look it)!

We don't even notice that the sun has come up as we've been cuddling and talking all night on the sofa until Alixe and Jerry (that's his name!) trot back downstairs for coffee and breakfast. Where did the time go? It was past noon and Alixe wanted to get Jerry out fast. Tony held my hand, kissed me goodbye and thanked me for the night of "dancing, great conversation and company" and strode off with my business card (with my email, cell number and office number) safely in his pocket.

I was still in shock, still feeling the warmth of his kiss on my lips as he drove off when Alixe gave me one of her "we need to talk, girlfriend" looks and we sat down to do that endless analysis of the evening. She was thrilled that I'd had fun and surprised at who I'd ended up with. According to her, there had been lots of other guys watching Tony and me dancing, waiting for a chance to ask me, but I hadn't even noticed. After all, it was my first time out in years and before that, it had been with Jeff, so I had little memory of being out and single.

Twelve hours! We had *actually talked* for 12 hours! He had been so easy to talk to, gently asking questions and seemingly very forthcoming with information about himself. Alixe's eyes twinkled mischievously when she asked how he had been - in bed?! I looked at her, bewildered, trying to explain that we'd just talked all night. She gave me that pitying look that you'd give someone when you either think they were giving a pathetic excuse or you can honestly believe that it is pathetically true. "Glad you had fun girl, but you have to realize that you probably won't hear from him," she sympathized. I didn't know what to expect or believe, but I knew that it had been a special, magical evening. And who knew, Pollyanna-that-I-am, maybe something would come of it?

9

Back home after taking a taxi back to my car still parked behind the jazz club, I settled back into the gloom of what had once been (I thought) a happy family home. The kids were up-and-about, glad to see me home and excited to hear about my sleepover at Alixe's. I told them that Alixe and I had gone out, met some friends and had fun - as much as they needed to know and be satisfied. I busied myself with Sunday dinner for the 3 of us - their father was going to be "out for the evening", he'd told them to tell me. That was just fine with me...the kids and I could have our regular routine without the discomfort of bristly interaction between their father and me.

After home-work was done and checked, piano and guitar were practiced, and we'd had great fun romping in the backyard with Jack (our rambunctious, goofy and loveable Jack Russell), it was time for bed. Our usual round of 3 bed-time stories (one chosen by each of them, one by me), they reluctantly settled down to their rooms. Stories were read in the family bed (now mine) and David (our oldest) stayed up his extra hour reading. (He was 3 years older than our youngest, Jackie, who nodded off more easily than usual into dream-land).

As I finished off the dinner dishes and made lunches for school the next day, the house seemed so quiet. Sweet Jack, ever faithful, sat by my feet as I did the dishes. He had sensed the changes in the house, watchful of the kids and diligent in his attention to me.

Before the split, he had been relegated to the main floor and slept in the kitchen/family room behind closed doors because of STB-ex's "allergies". I had liberated Jack the day we called it quits to have his freedom of the whole house and he relished sleeping with me on the bed at night. I will never forget that look of guilty pleasure on Jack's puppy-face that first night, as I called him upstairs to snuggle with me. He had joyously curled his warm puppy-body against my back, stretching and sighing delightedly. It was where he had always belonged.

When I wearily made my way to bed that night after checking on the kids, I thought about how their worlds had been turned upside-down. They looked so peaceful as they slept, but I knew that Jackie was plagued with bad dreams, as she had often wandered into my room at nights since the night we split. David had been more stoic about it, mumbling he had "seen it coming" and I had seen him withdraw to his own company more and more. My mind wandered back to what had lead up to that fateful day...

Jeff had begun to spend less and less time at home and little with the family about 2 years before. The kids would bemoan the fact that "Dad never comes out with us anymore" to the places I had bought family passes for - the zoo, the science center, the heritage center, the amusement park, the family sports center with its pool. I had taken to swimming or skating or playing badminton/basketball/court sports at the sports center every

Sunday with the kids and many nights of the week when they had no home-work or other activities. We had our favorite urban park nearby that we'd bike through all spring and summer - 10 bridges spanning a lovely creek and a park filled with wildlife. As soon as the frost was gone, the kids and I would get our bikes ready for our evening or weekend bike jaunts. We couldn't wait for spring to come. Jeff used to come, but no more. In winter, I'd haul them on their toboggans to nearby sledding hills with Jack in tow, riding with his ears flying on each of their toboggans in turn. A nearby school had a great outdoor skating rink and we'd trundle over there with hot chocolate in a thermos to whirl on the ice or slap a puck around. Jeff used to skate, but had never bought a pair since we had been together, so he missed out on the fun.

We (the kids and me) had our own favorite hiking trail we'd take every late spring/early summer to climb up "our mountain" and as they grew each year, we'd get higher and higher up. That year, we had made it up to the top and saw the beauty of our world below us: miles and miles of coniferous forests, lakes, and rivers. The view was breathtaking. There were many preparations to make for this annual outing - bottles of water and juice boxes to be packed in our back-packs, our own home-made trail-mix we created from the bulk-foods section of the grocery store (nuts, raisins, some chocolate treats, sesame sticks...our own concoction, different every year), some fruit and wraps I made with their favorite meat and/or vegetable fillings. Everything we consumed, the packaging went back into the back-packs to help maintain the pristine beauty of our surroundings and be recycled at home. We always made 4 baggies of the trail-mix, one for each of us and one for a bear, in case we "met one" and it chased us. Silly, I know, and it probably wouldn't have helped if we did encounter a bear, but it added to the suspense and the thrill of our adventure. Jack would always lead the way, enthusiastically racing ahead of us and enjoying his share of the healthy goodies we had packed (except for the chocolate!).

Doing pretty well with all of the kid-stuff with school (driving them there and back), activities (sports, music, drama, voice lessons for Jackie, play-dates with friends), volunteering at their school, and all of their activities was wonderful but also exhausting. I wouldn't have missed that time with them for anything in the world. Jeff had "allergies" to dust so he couldn't help with maintaining the inside of the house and "allergies" to pollen and grass so he couldn't help with the gardening or the garage. He showed little interest in dear Jack, so he, too was my responsibility. All this with a full-time business and I was beyond stretched. Colds would turn into flus, into bronchitis and pneumonia and still I would plug through. Doctor's, specialists', dentists' appointments, parent-teacher meetings, recitals and games were all mine to keep up with the kids. He didn't even know their doctors' names, their coaches or most of their teachers.

I had tried valiantly to make "couple time" and dates for us - the kids loved seeing us dressed up and going out, but the arrangements were always mine to make. The same went for gifts - for the kids, for my family, for his family - mine to choose, wrap and get him to sign the card. He showed no interest and I made excuses to everyone. One day I had more than an epiphany when Jackie (then 7 years old) said to me: "Mom, you love David and me a lot, right?" "Of course," I replied. "How do you know?" I asked. She replied with a twinkle in her eye: "Because you always do things for us and buy us stuff". "Mom, you love Daddy a lot, right?" she continued. "Of course," I replied, wondering where this was going. "Because you always do things for Daddy and buy him things," she observed. Then that little beauty zapped me right between the eyes with: "Don't love yourself, do you Mom? You never do anything for yourself or buy anything for you!"

I was dumbfounded and stammered that "yes" I did, I had just bought some new shoes for myself a while back. Jackie gave a triumphant nod of her head as if I'd made her point and I resolved to myself that it was time to be a role-model for the kids. I was worthy, too and obviously needed to show them and me that I deserved more respect.

I had tried a couple of years before to talk to Jeff about things, but they were "fine" according to him. Our secretaries and assistants at the office were becoming increasingly uncomfortable at work (they told me, as we were all women except for Jeff), and they asked me if anything was wrong. We (he and I) rarely talked at work and had separate clients in our very busy, successful PR firm. Then, I had discovered that Jeff had secretly taken on a part-time contract working for another firm without telling me about it. I had seen mail coming to him from the firm and asked him about it. He defended himself, saying it was all for the greater good and all was fine. Staff started telling me that he was increasingly having people pay him in cash, instead of having our assistant bank the cheques and credit card dues at the end of the day. Something was up, but my blind trust after so many years together kept me ignorant and naïve to what he was ultimately doing. After all, he seemed to trust me with everything else, why shouldn't I be able to trust him with one thing?

Talking was getting us nowhere at work, at home, even on "dates" we always talked about work or the kids. I decided to try writing him a letter about how I was feeling and what I saw happening. One of my girlfriends told me that she had tried it with her husband and it really seemed to help their communication. So, I did it and he wrote back a letter that ignored everything I'd said but implored me to keep on trying, not to leave him and he'd try harder. I never had said anything about leaving him, there were no ultimatums in it. The response shocked me, because all I'd asked for was for us to work on things. To even think of or hear of one or the other of us giving up and splitting was something I'd never even considered or

Imagined could ever happen. So, things continued the same as they had been, and nothing changed, no matter how I tried. I felt like I continued to bang my head against a wall...

That year, I turned 40 and Jeff ignored it - no celebration, no party, no get-togethers. Hurt, I asked him what was going on. He was hurt, he said, because on his birthday (10 days before mine), the kids and I had sent him on a spa-day for a massage and pampering and then we took him out for a lovely dinner. Apparently, he hadn't wanted to spend the day away from the family, he said (although he rarely chose to spend time with any of us any other time) and he had been hurt so he chose to hurt me back by ignoring my birthday! I was stunned - how childish! My girlfriends were infuriated and disgusted, but I was in too much shock to react and put my head down to keep plugging away.

Like everything else, I planned the family vacations for summer and holidays and that year, we were going to New York. The kids had always wanted to go, but I had come down with a cold, then bronchitis and could barely talk for coughing on the trip. They loved it, but when we got home I got sicker and sicker until I could hardly breathe and was exhausted even waking up. The walk-in doc (my secretaries marched me down to the clinic despite my protests) said it was "walking pneumonia" (my 2nd time) and I needed to rest but I still couldn't stop coughing. It took months to recover, as there was no way I could slow-down from trying to keep everything together.

That year, Jeff had planned a surprise party for me for my 41st with the help and bullying of my friends to make up for the year before. I came home from grocery shopping to unload and put away everything by myself as always, dressed like a mess to a darkened house and no one to help me. That was no surprise. Hot and sweaty, I turned on the lights and was greeted with "surprise!" and the kids and my friends looked expectantly at my exhausted face. Jeff stood there looking self-satisfied and smug, a smirk on his face. As I circulated around the room to the well-wishes of my friends, some of my girlfriends looked a little anxious and asked me to "talk in private" later. When I'd done the rounds and made sure everyone was eating, drinking and merry-making, I signaled my buddies to meet me on the back deck.

The first thing they all said was: "Did you see that's she's here? Did you see what she's wearing? You should see them together!" I stared at them all blankly. Alixe explained that they had all been watching Jeff cozying up to Julia, a woman he had befriended while out consulting in the community. He had mentioned mentoring her and helping her with her business over lunches and I had been happy to see him giving back to the community. She was, after all, a single mom trying to grow her party-planning business to help support her and her kids. It seemed like a nice change-of-pace for Jeff to help someone, but I had noticed he seemed to be working later and later all the time, "at the office" on weekends and rarely making it to the school or extra-curricular events for the kids...I had bought him a new motorcycle that year and he frequently took it on rides by himself on the weekends, although I had been hoping we could get back into riding together like we had as grad students many years before.

"He's been too cozy with her since we got here to help set things u," Alixe explained. "They giggle with each other, she brushes up against him and they keep making in-jokes. Jeff hasn't even talked with the husbands yet, he's been so pre-occupied with her," said Lucy, my friend of many years since grad school.

I poo-poohed that it was nothing other than friends. In response, Sarah, Janie, Jessica, Lucy and Alixe collectively rolled their eyes and sighed in exasperation. "Has he even given you the combination to the safe yet?" asked Sarah, who I had befriended as our kids went to the same school together. They were referring to a safe that had been in the basement when we bought the house 8 years before. Even after repeated questioning, Jeff never had the time to tell me or show me how to get into it. It hadn't seemed like a big thing, as our finances were altogether, weren't they? Nevertheless, I spent the rest of the night watchful of Jeff and Julia's interactions. They did seem to be in the same place at the same time a lot and I caught a few meaningful glances between them. She seemed to avoid any eye-contact with me and never did say goodbye to me when she left near the end of the evening. When I mentioned it to Jeff, he looked uncomfortable as he explained that she had to leave quickly because her babysitter had to leave earlier than expected.

Life had continued along busily. Jeff left unexpectedly one Sunday afternoon without mentioning what he was doing or where he was going. When he returned that night, he told me that Julia's house had been burglarized and he had gone to help her out with the police. The crooks had even taken much of the food from her freezer, so I wrote him a cheque to give to her to help refill her freezer. It had been a busy day with taking the kids to baseball and soccer games (both at the same time, trying to drive back-and-forth to watch as much of both as I could), and I was tired but thought it was time to talk. Jeff didn't think so - he went to his home-office with a drink and I dragged myself to bed after making lunches, getting back-packs ready for school the next day and doing one more load of laundry. I lay in bed, my body exhausted but my brain in overload.

Why the secrecy? Why the lack of communication? We never seemed to talk or spend any time together anymore, whether as a family or heaven-forbid as a couple. He was always "too busy", making excuses to the kids and me. I was forever going to events by myself and the kids were so often upset as we trotted off to our favorite places on our family passes - minus one family member. I had become mom-and-dad and they hardly ever invited Jeff to their events anymore, anticipating excuses and disappointment. Weekends were spent without him around, many nights he'd come home when we were all in bed. For lunches at work, he went out every day. He never seemed to be around anymore. Our only "intimacy", if you could call it that, was when he'd frequently roll me over in the middle of the night and do-his-thing in the dark with me half-asleep. Awakened from my exhaustion, I was too tired to protest and only years later began to see it for what it was: a further invasion of my trust, my dignity, my very being.

Chapter 2: In the Beginning

Jeff and I had met at grad school doing our MBAs. I had completed my first degree out west and with my top grades, had my choice of programs across North America but chose an eastern-version of Canadian ivy-league school because of the profs there. Jeff had studied at a top school out east, where he was from and his dad had been a professor. We met in my second week there away from home. It was at a "grad smoker" and his quick wit, sense of humor and avante-guard dress (I later learned it was because he was color-blind) drew me to him. There were many other guys interested, but he kept the evening going by suggesting everyone go out to a late-night restaurant after the party ended, then back to his apartment to continue the party. We had lunch the next day at school and then our first date. He insisted that he didn't like to mix his personal with his school life, so that we should keep our dating to ourselves and I had no problem with that. We went to visit his parents for the first time much later, although we visited Toronto frequently on our own together.

It was all such a whirlwind. When I did meet his parents, they accepted and treated me as one of the family and I couldn't help but fall in love with them, too. His dad would even go out to buy me specialty coffees when we visited, although Jeff never drank coffee at that time and he bemoaned having to endure the world's worst, dustiest tea-bags to drink. His mom and I cooked together, and we had become like best friends, but his sister despised me from day one. On our first family meal together, she made fun of my outfit, called me a "large Western woman", and proceeded to diagnose me as "clearly repressed" because of my love of heavy-metal music. Jeff said she was just jealous of how well her mom and I got along but it was unsettling...

Meanwhile back at school, I maintained several jobs, as I had always done all through my school years, this time as a research and a teaching assistant, completing my class work by the end of my first year. Jeff and I won major scholarships and I helped him on his classes. I began spending more and more time at his place, even calling my parents on my regular Sunday night calls back to home from his place. That spring, my parents announced that they were coming to visit with my little brother for 2 weeks, staying at my place. I panicked, knowing that now was the time for them to meet Jeff. I had mentioned him in our calls and in my visit back home for Christmas, but not how close we had become or that we were virtually living together.

My family arrived at my tiny 1-bedroom apartment, my parents to stay in my room and my brother to stay on the sofa-bed in my living-room. I announced that I was staying at my friend Wendy's (actually at Jeff's) to give them some space and made dinner for us all, with Jeff to come by for coffee and dessert after dinner. To say that the meeting between Jeff and my parents didn't go well was an understatement - he was argumentative and obnoxious, putting his feet up on my coffee-table (no one sat in the living-room at my parents' home as it was a show-piece, let alone put up their feet on the coffee-table!), wearing his dingiest sweat-pants and socks with holes in them. My parents were less-than-impressed and after he and I had left separately, they called me at his place later that night (guess they had remembered his name, after all!) to say they needed to meet me at a local hotel at noon the next day, as they were leaving. Not an auspicious beginning...

The meeting was a fiasco. Not only did they not approve of him, they insisted that I either come home with them or break off my relationship with Jeff. I argued that it was my life and my future, that they'd just have to deal with it and they retaliated that they would never let my brother visit me if I was with Jeff and they would have no contact with me until I broke it off. In a way, they pushed me even further towards him without realizing it, as I would never give up my future career and education, let alone my autonomy. My parents and I didn't speak for months afterwards, although I continued to write letters imploring them to reconsider.

Unbeknownst to me until about a year after we got together, Jeff had been married before and no one had told me. I found out at a concert Wendy (my student "pen-pal" and mentor) and I attended together in Montreal one weekend. We took an all-inclusive bus-trip there and got pretty liquored-up before the concert, when she told me what she had heard: he had been married, had a child, they lost the child and they divorced.

What?! Arriving from the bus-ride home back at his place, I confronted him with what Wendy had told me. He quietly went to a drawer and took out a picture of his wife and baby son, told me he had died and there was a part of him that I would never know or be able to reach. He wouldn't tell me anymore and I struggled to find out more from friends and colleagues at school. Turns out they had met back at school and married soon after. The pregnancy was unexpected, and the baby had died unexpectedly a few months later. They all said Jeff had been a great and loving father and was devastated when they lost the baby. His wife had a break-down and they split soon after. When I had met him, he was still grieving.

Trying to broach the subject again with Jeff, he was a closed book. How had he been before? Did he ever want to have children again? His parents were not allowed to speak of their lost grandchild or have any pictures up of him and I thought how sad it was for them not to be able to share this with me. Yet I soldiered on, convinced that my unconditional love and caring would make Jeff whole and happy again...

We bought a house together while still in grad school. I cashed in some of my RRSPs and Canada Savings bonds to make the down-payment, not wanting to rent anymore and to have a place together. We nested in our new home and got engaged 2 years after meeting. His proposal was, like him, unusual as we decided to have our 2nd anniversary together at home with a home-made "gourmet" dinner. For dessert, he brought out a big box with smaller and smaller boxes inside them until the final, tiny one which was a jewelry box. He got down on his knee and proposed and we toasted our engagement with Canadian bubbly. The call to my parents to tell them was stilted and uncomfortable, but his parents were thrilled.

I planned most of the wedding myself, putting on-hold a simple cream satin gown I had found on sale. My parents had called to see what the plans were and when I told them, my mother got on the line to say that she really wanted me to wear her wedding-dress and my father said they were paying for everything except for the photographer. That call was more than a surprise, but I went with it and got the best deals I could, just like the plans I had been making before. Even with 75 people in attendance, I was able to keep the budget under $5,000.

It was a bit of a fiasco the night before, as my mother got drunk and belligerent with me at the party we held at our house for out-of-town guests, but she had brightened up by our wedding-day and told Jeff ("sonny-boy") to call her "Mom". Even as I have looked back at the pictures over the years, I can see the strain on my parents' faces and Jeff's discomfort in the shot of him dancing with my mother. As I had never told my parents about Jeff's previous marriage and divorce (he already had enough strikes against him in their eyes), it was tense when his best friend and Best Man gave his speech, but he thankfully avoided the subject.

Life went along as I got my first job out-of-town while finishing off my degree and Jeff was still working on his. I rented a room in an elderly lady's house for 4 days a week, working 12-hour days to get home for long-weekends at home together with Jeff. I helped him the best I could to finish off his degree and he got a job in the town where I worked, so we sold our first home together and bought a new one out in the country outside of town. It was beautiful there...14 acres of a tree farm where you could wander for hours amid paths I mowed through berry patches, winding around a creek. The drive to work was over half-an-hour, but the seclusion and beauty of our surroundings was worth it. I dug out a quarter of an acre to make a vegetable garden, planting tomatoes, peppers, eggplant, corn, carrots, and radishes. After that, I added a huge herb garden filled with dill, mint, basil, oregano, and many others. It was all within a few steps of our front door.

Our little home had been built by a boiler-maker and was situated among the trees, heated by hot water through pipes that could either be fueled by natural gas or wood from our land. Running through the middle of the house was a staircase up made of beautiful pine boards and banisters, and a similar one down. Our basement was unfinished, but I wanted to give us more room to grow, so I developed a plan to finish the basement into a rec room with a 3-piece bathroom. I had learned to do some renovating and use basic tools from my father and uncle, and I bought all of the materials so that we could do it ourselves. With my direction, we framed in the rooms, put up pine wall-board and tile, and only needed a plumber to plumb in the shower, toilet, and sink we had bought for the little bathroom down there. We also renovated the upstairs main bathroom, adding in a 6-foot soaking tub and a huge picture window beside it to be able to look out at our trees from the tub. No one could see us, as it was totally private with any neighbors living miles away.

About a year after moving there, I developed many of the symptoms of pregnancy and I went to visit my family doctor. After a negative result on the pregnancy test, she diagnosed a urinary tract infection, but we were disappointed at the negative pregnancy result. Jeff and I discussed if we were ready to be parents and I asked him how he would cope with having another child after he had lost his first one. He simply said that he wasn't sure and would either run in terror at the child-birth or "deal with it". He said he was ready, so we decided to try.

I seem to know my body pretty well and knew I was pregnant within a couple of weeks. Sure enough I was, and Jeff and I were thrilled when we found out for certain. After the ultra-sound when we found out it was a boy, I asked him how he would deal with having a second son and he just said he'd have to and that was it. His parents had moved from Toronto to be near us and we prepared for the birth. My parents were to come a couple of weeks later, although they were invited to be there for the birth, as well. It turns out, as I discovered years later, that my mother felt very left-out with Jeff's parents moving nearby, as if she had been side-lined but that had never been my intention. It played a much bigger part in the years ahead...

Six months into the pregnancy, I was sick...sick beyond morning sickness, and was unable to hold any food down. My sister-in-law was visiting from Toronto. She was a physician now and followed me into the bathroom, shocked at all of the blood that poured out of me as I peed. She told my husband to rush me to hospital immediately, where they discovered that I wasn't losing the baby, but had a virulent UTI. They kept me in hospital for 2 weeks with a fetal heart monitor on my stomach to ensure that the bay was healthy. I was unfortunately placed on the maternity ward and saw and heard mothers coming back and forth with their babies from the nursery nearby. I was desolate, but the nurses who looked after me assured me that they would be there when I gave birth to my healthy baby. And they were right...

The birth of David was a big one for the family...the first grandchild for my parents and for his parents, as far as everyone else knew.

Our best friend Jackie (who worked with Jeff) was there for the birth, thankfully, because Jeff wouldn't leave the top of the bed to see David come into this world. Jackie's face became ashen after David screamed his way into the world, pink and beautiful, as I hemorrhaged out-of-control. They said they almost lost me there and I was sent home too soon, passing out (thankfully with David in his crib) from an infection they had missed. My loving in-laws happily helped out until my family arrived and everyone fell in love with David...round, alert and lusty as he ate non-stop on-demand. I had decided to breast-feed and loved it as much as he did, but my father (and mother) were uncomfortable with it and would ask me to leave to room, to do it in private. My brother Garry (8 years younger than me) held David like a football the first time he held him, terrified to drop him but was thrilled to have a little buddy he could nurture to be a Dallas Cowboys fan like his uncle.

Although I had planned to take a year-long maternity leave from work, Jeff came home soon after David's birth to say he had been fired, along with his boss. It was a shock and a huge blow to our future, but I agreed to go back to work after 5 months home while Jeff stayed home with David and looked for another job. In the meantime, we lived off of the money from my maternity payments. I wasn't ready to leave David and return to work, but I had to because living on a maternity income with no other income was impossible. Time stretched on as Jeff couldn't find any work in Ontario and he announced one day that we were moving to

Saskatchewan, as they were looking for professionals to work in the government and would pay our move and all expenses. He had done an interview over the phone with them and they said there was work for me there, too. So, we packed everything up, including his parents, put both of our houses up for sale, and moved.

Jeff had been given a higher-management position in HR and I was slated for the same in Regina, which was a 35-minute commute for me each way every day. David's daycare was just up the street from our house and it broke my heart every time to have to say goodbye on my way to work, but he quickly adapted and was happy there. He was such a sociable little guy.

About 6 months after beginning my job in Regina, another job came up near our home with the government, just up the street from our house there. I applied for it and got it, so life was better because I could visit David on my lunch-hours. Both Jeff and I got evening positions teaching extension courses for the University of Regina and we were making friends in town and with other professionals in Regina. We even started up a gourmet club with our new-found friends and my in-laws were thrilled to make many friends in town, as well. We were closer to my family (at least physically), and we settled happily in the warm, friendly little city.

With David now 2, I asked Jeff if he was ready to have another child, as I had heard that 3 years apart was a really good spacing of children. At first, he said that he didn't know, maybe one was enough, but I explained that being an only child was tough, having been one myself for 8 years. After thinking about it he agreed, and we got pregnant with Jackie. David had been a very verbal, quick-to-develop little one and he would talk for hours to my growing tummy, telling his little sister (we had found out it was a girl) how he was going to play with her, to help feed her and sing to her. Life was again feeling settled and then Jeff came home one day to tell me that he had been fired (again, who gets fired from a government job?!). My world upside-down again and pregnant, he announced that he had been looking further west and was researching jobs in British Columbia.

Unbelievable...here I was again, pregnant, enjoying some stability, career success, family and friends and to have to move...again? Well, Jeff interviewed for a higher management job in a small town and got it. Jackie was born a month before we had to move, again with Jackie (the children's god-mother) at the business-end. Like her brother David, Jackie was the biggest in the nursery, weighing in at almost 10 pounds and almost always ravenously hungry. David took to being a big brother with his usual aplomb and adored his little sister.

We flew into Vancouver with a 1-month-old infant, a toddler, and my elderly in-laws and stayed at a motel in the middle of nowhere, near the town we were to live in. There was one grocery store, 2 cafes, a motel and hotel and cold, watchful eyes everywhere. We quickly found a big-old-house nearby in town and a duplex for my in-laws and I set about making drapes for the whole house, trying to settle in and make it home. I got David into an area play-school and tried to fit in, inviting other kids for play-dates but their parents always politely refused. Even when I took him skating on the local rink with Jackie in her stroller in-tow, the rink always cleared out, with no one to be seen.

I spent my time at my in-laws' and the local grocery store, where they served up free coffee and cookies for the kids. It was a lonely life, as we could only afford one car and the best I could do to give David some peers was to drive 45 minutes once-a-week to a small city nearby, where I had signed him up for a gym class. Our treat on those days was lunch at the local McDonald's and a wander around the mall.

My sweet father-in-law had a stroke while he and my mother-in-law were on holiday in California so when they got back home, I helped her with him as he was more than a handful. He had a second and final stroke a few months later while David was at a pre-school recital. Jeff began to withdraw and wouldn't let me reach him, so I became even lonelier than ever.

I began to look for work somewhere, although I had hoped to stay home with the kids until they were both in school. Thankfully, I found a part-time position to join a firm in a town a half-hour away, as Jeff was informed that he was being let-go (again!) effective in a few months. I knew I had to take over being the provider again, so I began to look for work in Vancouver and found a great part-time position there with a big firm. The only thing was, the commute from town to Vancouver would be over an hour-and-a-half and I knew I couldn't do that with the kids still in town, so I suggested we move to a closer small city for Jeff to look for work from there.

So, after I commuted to Vancouver for over a month, we moved (along with my mother-in-law) to a newly-built house in a smaller city nearby. It was a lovely town and the people were much more welcoming. David and Jackie loved the daycare near home there and he made many friends in the kindergarten he attended. My mother-in-law blossomed, making friends in town and writing for the local newspaper and I started a column there, myself. The only down-side was that she and I would butt-heads when it came to parenting, and she would become the kids' lawyer when I tried to discipline them. Jeff would remain neutral in those weeks when we didn't talk, she and I, but we would eventually make up. I loved her too much to stay angry with her and understood that what she was doing was out of love.

The kids loved having their grandmother so close-by. She was a wonderful grandmother but parented differently than me and when she interfered, it made things very tense, as I felt she was undermining my authority, as well as the kids' respect for me. Even as I hated disciplining them, I knew I had to (Jeff and I had agreed that we would never use physical punishment) for them to be good people and respect authority figures. My mother-in-law's admonishments of me constantly made me look like the bad-guy and I hated it.

In the meantime, my mother had withdrawn further, and my parents never visited when Jackie was born but she started to write and send parcels to the kids when Jackie was about a year old. We decided to visit my family for Mother's Day when Jackie was almost 2 and David was almost 5. On the drive into town, I called the house just to let them know we were in town, but my brother answered in hysteria. My mother had been taken to hospital in an ambulance and we raced there to see her. When we arrived, we found my father and brother weeping and the nurses told me she had died...her "heart had exploded", so-to-speak. Jackie was never to see her grandmother alive and the dress my parents had bought her on their trip to Spain she wore to the funeral. My little family (my mother's older sister and her husband, my beloved uncle and god-father) was devastated and my father and brother were totally lost, wandering around as if in a bad dream. Jeff was lost to me at this time, as well. He kept his distance, trying to find work. The only good thing that came of this terrible time was that my father and I became very close as he struggled to find his way again without his beloved Joan.

Back home, I couldn't take much time off work and threw myself back into being a wife and mother, an adult-daughter and friend to my father, with my mother-in-law there for me gladly along the way. I found a good job for Jeff part-time with my firm in Vancouver and we also opened up our consulting firm together. My part-time position in the small town was becoming strained, as many of the accounts coming in wanted to work with me, so my partner and I parted ways and Jeff and I decided to move to Vancouver, to be closer to work and so the kids could be in daycare and school closer-to-home. I had been terrified if one of them had become ill and I was far away, taking too long to get to them.

In the midst of all this, my beloved mother-in-law had a stroke and ended up in hospital in Vancouver, with me running back-and-forth with the kids to visit her and encourage her as she recuperated and took physio- and speech therapy at the hospital there. It became clear that having her live with us would put an even greater strain on me, as I knew somehow that Jeff would provide little help. So, I made the difficult suggestion to have her move into a lovely new Lodge close to our home and right near the kids' school. She was fine with it and looked forward to meeting new friends, but I know that Jeff was not happy about it. However, I was already spread too thin and my mother-in-law knew it, understanding that her son would have been no help in taking care of her.

The children and I added daily visits to their grandmother and I would bring her back home for days and evenings. It was wonderful to still have her in our lives. I would take the kids for lunch to visit her from school and after-school and have her over on weekends, running back-and-forth to the lodge when her oxygen tank was running out. I like to think that she had a full life with her grandchildren in her life, and she happily joined into new activities like painting classes and made many new friends at the lodge. But she had her final stroke during a visit to our house soon after we returned from a trip with friends, after kibitzing with me in the garden while I re-potted plants as Jeff was out barbecuing dinner. We raced after the ambulance to the hospital, getting his brother and sister on the phone long-distance in the room to be able to say to her what they wanted to, to say goodbye. For 7 hours, the kids sat on either side holding her hands and telling her how much they loved her until she peacefully took her final breath. Jeff took the gold necklace from around her neck after she died and put it around Jackie's neck, still warm from her grandmother. He told her that she would still carry the warmth of her beloved grandmother. It was a heart-breaking time.

The funeral was tough. My mother-in-law's brother, who we hadn't seen in years since we visited Toronto, felt so guilty because he had made little effort to keep up with her. None of her sisters could make it, because they were all elderly and having health problems. My sister-in-law was her usual caustic self. And my brother-in-law...haven't mentioned him yet...was all about show-me-the-money.

My brother-in-law is younger than Jeff and had been having trouble "finding himself" when we met. He was on social assistance, living off his mother's credit-card in a basement apartment in Toronto when I told Jeff we needed to do something to help his parents with Norm. We had just bought our first house together and I suggested he come to live with us in the basement while he finished his degree and looked for work. He jumped at the chance and proceeded to destroy our basement with the bugs, dirt and filth he accumulated there. Behind my back, Jeff had lent him money to buy his first car and I said enough-was-enough. He had been fired from his first job but eventually found one in a non-profit organization in town and moved out. Then, he got his girlfriend pregnant and proceeded to call me to "ask her to have an abortion"...really? I refused, of course, but did talk to them about what their options were. They (unfortunately, in retrospect, and it wasn't my suggestion) decided to get married, although their relationship was a volatile and unhealthy one. She hardly ate during the pregnancy and survived mainly on diet pop...not a great beginning for my little nephew, who was born 6 months after David.

I felt sorry for my nephew, little Jason and set about having him visit for summers, taking him to and paying for camps with the kids and taking him on family holidays with us. His parents split when he was really little and he lived most of the time with my brother-in-law, who seemed more pre-occupied with other women than his son. More on that later...

Back to my mother-in-law's funeral, Jeff's sister Linda scoured our house for what she thought was hers. She tried to walk off with a painting I had bought Jeff for his 30th birthday in her purse. When she left for the airport after the funeral, we noticed that Jackie's necklace from her grandmother had gone missing. She had just taken it off to have a bath and couldn't find it. Linda called from the cab-ride to say that she had taken it...that it should have been hers. She asked me what was the right thing to do and I just shook my head, sighed and told her to do what she thought was right. She kept it. Typical. It was always all about her.

Life returned to normal, but my children and my husband were sad and lonely for my mother-in-law, as was I. The children would talk to me and I would tell them to talk to their grandma in their dreams and she would hear them, but Jeff was another case. He withdrew even further and wouldn't talk about it. His only connection with his family now was his brother and nephew and I struggled to keep that going, but one summer it was enough...

I had arranged for Jason to fly in and stay with us for the summer, to go on holiday with us to Tofino, then into a drama camp with David and Jackie when we returned. One day at work, I got a frantic call from David at his camp...had his father been married before, had he had a son before who had died, was he not his dad's first child? I told David to hold on, I'd be there soon. After telling Jeff about the call, I raced to the camp. David was hyper-ventilating and Jason was sulking. Norm had been visiting us at the time and he drove over too, after Jeff had called him. It was clear that the only way Jason could have found out was from Norm, who said it wasn't either his or Jason's fault (big surprise!).

David, Jackie and Jason had their recital to do, so we watched agonizingly as they finished their performance. I brought the kids back to the office (I had cancelled my clients after the call) and put Jackie into our kid-room with a video to watch while David sobbed his heart out, rocking on my lap. Eventually, Jeff came in and told him the same story he had told me years before...he was married before, had a son, he had died, he and his first wife divorced, and he had married me and had David and Jackie. Then he left, taking Jackie home with him. I had told him years before that he needed to tell the kids one day before they found out the wrong way, but he hadn't listened and now David had paid the price. It broke my heart to see my son's anguish.

I held David in my arms as his little body was wracked with agony. He didn't know he had had a bigger brother, he felt that he wasn't his father's first child or son, did he love him as much...his misery, sadness and insecurity surrounded him as much as the love I tried to envelop him in. When he was calmer and we returned home for dinner, I was infuriated to find Norm at the dinner table with Jason, acting as if nothing had happened. I asked him if he had anything to say to David and he told Jason to tell him he was sorry...that was it! He then told him to bring his dinner to his room and stay there for the night.

Later that evening, after I had done the dinner dishes, Norm and Jason were out playing football (I had taught Jason to catch and throw, as his parents hadn't ever bothered) with Jeff and Jackie while David watched miserably. I told Norm that was an interesting way of disciplining a child...playing football with him and he rolled his eyes, sending him to his room at our house (again). When I was taking up a load of folded laundry, I found Jason sulenly playing video-games in the upstairs kids' play-room and told him that was not where he was told to be, that I didn't understand how he could be so mean to his cousin who had only ever been kind to him. He said that the other kids in the camp liked David more and he felt left-out, so he wanted to hurt him. He had managed to do so very well. After that, I refused to have Norm and Jason stay in our home anymore.

After the death of my mother-in-law, Jeff withdrew even further (if possible) and I continued to try to reach out to him, understanding his pain. The one time he did say something was that I didn't know what it was like to be "an orphan". I fully understood his sense of loneliness, but I had been there the whole time, trying to reach out to him and he always turned me away. I didn't know what to do anymore, so just kept trying to make everyone happy.

My poor father had been a lost soul since my mother's death and we frequently called each other. He came to visit for the kids' birthdays and Christmas when he could, loving being a grandfather. My brother had married and moved to the States for work, so Dad was all alone now. Having retired early for him and my mother to travel as much as possible, he still kept up with his co-workers, joining two groups of them who went out to lunch every month. It was then that he met up with an old neighbor from the past, my old violin teacher Arlene. Mom had hated her, finding her pretentious and fake but had never told that to my father. She was cultured, musical and flirtatious...putting her wiles on my father, who was smitten. I was happy that he had some companionship, someone he could enjoy music and outings with, but Dad surprised me one day with a call to ask me if I was okay with him asking Arlene to marry him. Shocked as I was, as Dad had always said that Mom had been his one true love, I quickly told him that if it made him happy, I was thrilled for him. He told me that when he had called Garry to ask him, Garry had refused to talk about it and had angrily hung up. I explained to Dad that Garry had never gotten over losing Mom and it would just take him some time, that I'd help him understand...

So, Dad flew the 4 of us back for their wedding. Jeff hadn't wanted to go, as his relationship with my Dad had always been strained.

Whenever Dad used to visit us, he would apparently pull Jeff aside and ask him to be a better husband, to take better care of me and not let me have to work so hard. I didn't know this until after the split when Dad told me, but he kept trying to make sure I was happy and okay. In the midst of all this, Dad had visited my Aunt and Uncle, telling them about his engagement to Arlene and my Aunt had kicked him out!!! She told him that if he had ever really loved my mother (and she doubted it), he wouldn't ever remarry. While she and Dad had never been particularly close, Dad and Uncle had always been like brothers and from then on, my aunt forbade Uncle from having anything to do with Dad…unbelievable! I tried many times (unsuccessfully) to broach the subject with my aunt and uncle over the phone and on my split-time visits back home (when I would rotate back-and-forth from Dad's to Aunty and Uncle's), but she would hear nothing of it. Uncle wouldn't take the inevitable nagging he'd receive if he tried to maintain the relationship. It was a sorry, sad state of affairs, but everyone had always seemed to give in to my aunt. She had won (again), isolating Dad and Uncle from the warm, loving relationship they had enjoyed since marrying into the family. With Dad's brother living far away in England and Uncle's brothers younger and pre-occupied with their growing families, the two had formed a strong bond, the sons my grandparents had never had but adored as their own. Amazing that as small as my family was, it was fractured even further…

Dad and Arlene's wedding was at her church that Dad used to

accompany her to on some Sundays. Her 2 daughters (I had grown up with them as neighbors, never really friends), my brother and me look at the camera with frozen smiles in the pictures I look back on. Their mother got a good deal...someone to take her on fancy vacations and to expensive restaurants that she never could before, and Dad had a companion to share his passion for music with, although her interests were classical and his were jazz. I rationalized to my brother that Dad had someone to enjoy life with once again, not just through his visits with us. He wasn't so convinced, and sadly at the end, Garry had been right...

Chapter 3: I Start to Make a Life for Myself

My friend Alixe, who I first met when we hired her as our Office Manager, had quickly become my best friend. With her brash wit and insightful observations about people, it was hard not to like her. A single mom, she worked hard and was a wonderful, loving parent to her son Nick, who was David's age. We would find time for lunches together when it wasn't busy at work and she, Nick, me and the kids began to go on family outings together.

Outside of other mothers whose kids attended my kids' school or outside activities, Alixe really became my only friend who I spent time with apart from the kids. She was a breath-of-fresh-air, always telling-it-like-it-is, her positive energy and attitude providing a refreshing new take on life. We had become friends not because we were moms, but because we thought alike in many ways, although her philosophy on life was in some ways counter- to my own and I needed it.

Somehow, I had grown up feeling responsible for and being wracked with guilt about everything and everyone. It was so much a part of me that I didn't even notice it until Alixe hit me with it one day. Always being the one to apologize for everything, even if it wasn't my fault, I'd even ask permission growing up at home to open the fridge and get a glass of milk, for heaven's sake. Alixe challenged me one day when I apologized for a client coming in late. "Enough, already! Everything isn't your fault!" she admonished me with exasperation. Her philosophy about life, that guilt was a "choice", and not a good one at that, really made me start to think. She began to encourage me to do things for myself, to believe in me. How busy our business was was not due to some fluke or luck, she reminded me, it was due to my hard work and how good I was at my job. I began to step back and really take a look at myself and my life, thanks to her and it didn't look good. Yet her patience and caring proved to be a great sounding-board that I had lacked, racing around to take care of everyone else.

I had taken on the mantle from a young age of making sure everyone was okay. When my grandfather had died unexpectedly in an accident, I had been the one to identify his body at the morgue, to protect my family from that horror. With my mother's increased drinking to dull the pain, I had taken it upon myself to help raise my brother, to make things as normal as possible. He had been born with a degenerative joint disorder that had only fuelled my mother's guilt and drinking even more, so I set about to protect him in the outside world where kids teased and tried to beat him up after school, as well as at home, where our mother was increasingly unpredictable. I had decided to try to help my grandmother after our grandfather's untimely death, driving her faithfully to his grave each week, my heart breaking as she fell to her knees every time, begging God to take her to her beloved husband of 65 years.

I had learned to drive as early as I could after Dad had to have life-threatening surgery when I was 15, no longer able to drive while he recuperated because Mom had never learned to drive. After he recovered I became her driver to her weekly grocery shopping trips, desperately trying to move things along as she rambled along, more times than not already half-cut. I realized that even with Jeff, I had tried to help him heal from his loss and improve his family relationships, taking care of his parents as we moved and until they died. It had become so much a part of me that it was inseparable...there seemed to be no me (other than professionally) outside of others.

Jackie's revelation about me not loving myself had really hit home as I looked at my life, focused so much on everyone else. As busy as I was trying to keep up with things, I had no hobbies or interests that I had maintained outside of what revolved around the family. I had noticed an advertisement in the paper about Tae Know Do classes for families at a school near our offices and suggested Jeff come with the kids and I to meet the Master to see what it was like. While he did come along to meet the Master and see the school, despite the kids' and my pleas to join along with us in family classes, he refused. So, the kids and I began classes 3 times a week and we loved it!!! Although I had been very athletic growing up and had actually attended a private boys' school for high-school on scholarship (they just started admitting girls there the year before I had applied), I had only continued sports in teaching and practicing with the kids since they were born. The rigorous conditioning was just what I needed and the self-discipline and self-respect the martial art promoted was good for the kids and me, as well. I started to blossom and both kids proved to be fast learners. Jeff resented the time we were away at the classes together, but he had his chance to join with us and hadn't wanted to…

The school had noon-hour adult classes and Alixe decided to join with me as well, so she and I would trot over there a couple of lunch-hours a week to work out and practice our growing skills. Most of the classes were comprised of kids and teens so I sometimes felt more than a little old, but the Master always went out of his way to encourage us and build up our confidence. He used to regularly ask the kids if they were "respecting your Mama?!" and tell them how proud they should be of me for working so hard. They loved the classes and the sense of family at the school and everyone used to get a kick out of watching little Jackie and me spar…like David and Goliath, as she was so fast with her foot-work and my big feet always seemed to get in the way. We would practice at home together, particularly before testing for our belts, and all three of us worked our way steadily up the ranks.

One of the young masters in particular, a young fellow who had been a high-level Red Belt when we had joined, took a great interest in teaching those of us "long-in-the-tooth", and Sammy would always make time after classes to help us figure things out. The coordination, of letting your muscle-memory flow and trusting your reflexes, channelling your mental and physical strength together, was a welcome focus for me to do something for myself after so many years. I became stronger and more self-confident in myself, other than as a wife, mother and business professional. My body became more toned and I built strong, healthy muscle mass. Jeff couldn't push me around as much anymore, and I began to stand up for myself in the business, not letting him make as many of the decisions on his own. I know now that this was the beginning of the end of things for us, as I had begun the process of finding and liking myself again. Dad was incredibly proud of me and cheered me on with each step I took.

The kids were just half a belt and one belt below me when it came time for me to test for my Black Belt. Sammy had worked so hard with me through the 4 years it had taken to get to that point and he was to test for his 2nd Dan at the same time. Jeff decided not to attend the testing and kept the kids at home, saying that it was to let me focus more, but I know that he was jealous of my new-found little martial arts family and the support and many friendships I had made there.

The testing session was long and gruelling, with almost the whole school quietly watching behind the glass walls of the waiting-room. The four of us (3 testing for Black Belts and Sammy testing for his 2nd Dan) all passed, and we congratulated each other for our hard work and dedication. When I returned home, the kids were so excited as I told them about it and Jeff sullenly retired to his office without as much as a "congratulations". He had already planted the seeds in the kids to both eventually quit Tae Know Do, telling them that if they didn't want to, they didn't have to continue on in classes. Eventually they both quit, David at his Black stripe level and Jackie at her Red Belt. They had loved it, but had begun to assert their growing independence more, choosing to quit many of their activities at their father's insistence.

Jeff was undermining me, encouraging the kids' inevitable assertion for independence and trying to isolate me from them. Little was I to know how much this would impact my relationship with the kids in the future, but I struggled on...

Work had become harder and harder...not the work itself, as I enjoyed the challenges and was good at it, but Jeff's and my relationship was becoming even more strained at work. Clients had begun to pick up on it, our assistants and secretaries wary of the coldness and brittle nature of our interactions at work. Jeff had insisted that we buy a lake house one summer and we took on the second mortgage of the little place we built by the lake. It was a lovely place where the kids and I would go fishing, have late-night fires in the fire-pit out back, build forts in the little forest of trees by the lake, do arts and crafts and puzzles together, cook and bake together. Jeff had started to bring his computer on our week-long summer holidays and weekend visits throughout the year there. The kids would chide him to come with us on our outings but most times he said he had too much work to do and should have stayed home but had to get his work done...

Little did I know that Jeff had not been keeping up with our taxes until one day he told me that we were late on them and had been assessed almost $20,000 in penalties!!! I was flabbergasted and terrified, as I had never known anything about it. He accused me of over-spending (athough I rarely spent anything on myself, everything I did spend was on him and the kids). I realized that all the time I was so busy with the kids, family and business, he was the one looking after the finances because I trusted him to. I began to take a look at our spending patterns and looking closely at credit card bills, saw that he had been spending a lot on lunches and dinners out ("business-related", he said), as well as many new racquets and equipment at his squash club ("new racquets don't last long anymore", he said). He said it might be time to sell the lake-house. I knew we were in trouble.

I had tried to show my support and interest in his passion for squash and when he said that he wanted to put Jackie in classes there and get her a coach, I had figured it was something they could share together. She was excited to share something with her father at the beginning, but began to get "headaches" or "tummy-aches" when I would go to drop her off for classes after school. It all became clear to me why when I attended a reception at a local bar after watching Jeff play in one of the club tournaments. He had, surprisingly, invited me to go and I had welcomed a chance to get dressed up for an evening together I hadn't had to plan. After we got there, an older gentleman I had never met before came up to me and asked me if Jeff was my husband. When I replied that he was, he proceeded to tell me not to let him train Jackie. Surprised, I asked him why and he replied: "Your husband has one of the worst tempers and breaks racquets by smashing them against the walls all the time. No one wants to play with him anymore and when you watch him play with your little girl, he is always yelling and screaming at her. It will break her spirit." I was shocked and felt so sorry for Jackie, then realized why she was having so many headaches and tummy-aches. When we returned home, I told Jeff that Jackie never seemed to want to go to the club anymore and it was time to let her quit. He accepted what I said sullenly and took her out of her classes but never did talk to her about it. When I told her she didn't have to go anymore, she was so relieved, she cried.

David, always a straight-A student, was becoming more sullen and quarrelsome. He would rarely do his homework anymore without an argument and started to drop out from his various extra-curricular activities. He didn't want to attend his private school anymore and insisted that he go to a public junior high close to our home. David had struggled with the social life of the kids' school, which we had decided to enrol the kids in when we had moved to Calgary because of the multiple-language programs. The problem was that as much as I had been involved in activities at their school, volunteering at events, in the library, lunch-hour hot-dog and chicken-nugget days, I was always an outsider. The other parents were very wealthy, the children dropped-off and picked-up by nannies while their mothers were at the spa. I had a couple of friends there, who like Jeff and I had enrolled their kids for the academic advantages, but we three were seen as the "earth-mothers" and sniffed at with disdain when we went to write down the kids' homework that was posted on the blackboard and pick up their backpacks each day after school. The teachers and secretaries loved us and our kids, wiping their tears after school-yard harassment or in the hallways, but they saw there was little we could do to fix things with their peers, even as we invited all their class-mates to birthday and Halloween parties.

I snapped one day after Jackie had been heart-broken at not being invited to one of her class-mates' parties. I saw her mother sitting with a table of her cronies having coffee at the local sports centre I had joined with the kids. I couldn't help myself and barrelled over to the table: "I understand that Vivian didn't invite Jackie to her party. Interesting that Jackie has always invited everyone to hers. Guess she'll end up being a bitch like her mother," I said loudly enough for everyone at the table to hear. Spoons dropped, jaws dropped, and no one said anything as I walked away to play basketball with the kids. I knew it was time to get the kids out of that school.

David had been harassed since he went there by one of the school bullies, a kid whose mother acted dumb about her kid's behaviour and always pleaded that it was provoked. He had jumped down from the stage in the gym, landing with an elbow on David's back, would throw rocks at him in the school-yard, break down his snow-forts, anything he could do when there were no adults around. The school always took the stance that if there were problems, David had to go tell a teacher but then nothing was ever done, anyway.

The last straw happened when I went to pick up the kids about a month before the end of the school-year. Jackie came running to the car breathlessly, telling me that David was in the office with a black eye. I ran to the office and found him there with a bag of ice over his eye, the bully sitting sullenly in the principal's office. The secretary, June, a lovely lady who knew too well the history of this dynamic, was watching over David who was trying valiantly not to cry. As I was asking how he was, the other mother came barrelling in. I shouted to the principal, who was in the office with her son, that he had better keep that bitch away from me or I'd finally do something about all this. The same went for her kid, I told him, as I was giving David my full permission to take matters into his own hands now. If the kid ever came anywhere near him again, David was to hit first and ask questions later and I didn't care what the repercussions would be. The principal assured me that it would never happen again and that there would be a 3-day suspension for the little monster. To be sure, I stood in the hallway the next day as the kids were arriving for class. The principal asked me what I was doing, and I told him I didn't trust that he was carrying through with the suspension, that I would be there each of the 3 days to make sure the kid wasn't at school. He shook his head and walked away but got his own back when I went to pick the kids up from school on the 3rd day. I had always volunteered to help for Sports Day but this year with the time I had taken off to patrol the halls, I had to catch up on my work and couldn't make it. When I asked the kids if they'd had fun, David said that he wasn't allowed to go, but had to sit in the office and write a 1000-word essay on how he had provoked the attack by the bully. That was it…I marched into the office and told the principal he was a coward and had never protected my children, neither of whom would be returning to the school the next week.

So, David started grade 8 at the local junior high and Jackie went into grade 5 in the area elementary school. Both were happy with the new friends they made at school and Jackie in particular had a wonderful teacher for the last month of the year and for grade 6 the next year. He took it upon himself to mentor her, suggesting she enter the educational program for gifted children and then into the junior high equivalent at David's school the next year.

David's achievement motivation reduced drastically when he got to the new school. I had expected an adjustment period, but he threw himself into his social life and began to hang-out with like-minded kids who showed no interest in school. Much as I tried to push him, tried working with the teachers to engage him in classes, Jeff just laughed and said it was just a "phase", refusing to help. He wouldn't come to parent-teachers and rolled his eyes when I reported back to him what the teachers had said and were trying.to do in order to help. As he saw it, he hadn't been a keener like me in high school and yet he managed to get advanced degrees and scholarships and David would do the same. I was on my own to fight every battle again.

Dad tried to reason with David when he would come to visit, patiently explaining what was expected of him. Hearing about and seeing David's change in attitude, Dad told him to shape up and show his mother more respect but David responded with silence, sullenness and resentment. Jackie started to follow suit and the tension in the house was becoming unbearable with my arguments with the kids to do their school-work. Behind his and my back, the kids started calling their beloved grandfather an "asshole", encouraged by Jeff, who told them Dad had said they deserved a good spanking. Maybe he had and maybe they did, but it was too late now.

Chapter 4: David

How to describe David, my first-born? He was the biggest baby in the hospital nursery when he was born, weighing in at 10 pounds. Big brown eyes, a shock of brown hair, he was so curious about the world around him from Day One. He seemed to eat non-stop and loved constant attention and stimulation. It is hard to even remember before David could walk, he tried climbing the kitchen drawers he had pulled out as stairs at 9 months old. He virtually toilet-trained himself by 13 months, really hating diapers, although he thoroughly enjoyed reading potty-training books with me on his little potty. Everyone at the day-care loved him, he was the first to greet everyone who came to visit and made friends easily.

Little David's hair had grown so long by age 1 ½ that the day-care ladies had started to French-braid it, so I knew it was time for his first hair-cut, a traumatic experience for both of us!!! He loved all sorts of books and was reading by age 4, especially after he saw his first National Geographic...he just wanted so much to be able to read the picture captions on his own.

David was an exuberant joy to be around and always full of fun. From early on, even after having to go back to work early after his birth, I would take a long lunch on Tuesdays to have lunch with him every week. That turned in to rotating lunches with each kid after Jackie was born. Precociously agile and coordinated, I coached David and his team in T-ball when he was 3 ½ and then he wanted to play soccer like my Dad. A star was born!!! Even on the small fields for the youngest players, David would easily score goals from far in his end. He had a boot on him!!! Arriving at the field and watching the team assembling, there were always chants of "David, David, David!", as he was consistently the top scorer. That passion for sports later included lacrosse and football, but more on that later…

As I often had music playing with the kids right from birth, David decided early on that he wanted to learn to play music, so I researched early-childhood musical programs and he and I began a program together when he turned 3. It began with learning the beat and activities to promote musical appreciation, then the children went on to learn the keyboard. David stayed at it for a year, then wanted to take guitar. I found a teacher nearby and he began with an acoustic, then an electric guitar, but getting him to practice was a night-mare, ending with either him or me (or both of us) frustrated and crying. His teacher explained that while David was a quick-study, without practice the classes were only practice for him. We mutually decided to take a break from guitar and a year later, David decided he wanted to play the violin, so I found a teacher, rented him an adorable ½-size violin and he began in earnest. Again, his practice waned, and he decided to "take a break" from it. His father had never shown any interest in it, so was no help at all.

Socially, everyone loved David…his teachers, the kids' parents in school, his coaches, everyone. The problem was his peers. His mind always seemed to be running a mile-a-minute and he "got things" so fast that school was often boring for him. He was happy to be a "teacher's helper" working with kids in school who needed help with reading or math, but became known as a "science geek" because of his fascination with so many things. While he was so popular at all of his activities with the kids there, school was a very demoralizing place for him. I struggled to try to set up play-dates, asking parents if their kids wanted to come over and play. David, like so many gifted kids, was miles ahead intellectually but at the same pace with his age-group emotionally, maybe even a little behind socially due to lack of experience with peers. The girls in school adored him because he was so kind and helpful, but the boys only seemed to like having him on their teams because of his athletic skills and were mean or belittled him otherwise.

I worked hard to engage David in all sorts of activities, like I did later with Jackie. He would learn to horse-back ride, play every sport, learned fencing in camps, took swimming lessons, I tried everything with him musically, and he really enjoyed the drama camps I enrolled him and Jackie in for part of each summer. He loved to draw his own humorous cartoons, so I found a class for kids at the College of Art in cartooning and he loved that. I took a landscape painting class I had found at the same time as his class on Saturdays and together, we would often do our art-work.

David had a passion for animals and their welfare. At an early age, he read an article about PETA (People for the Ethical Treatment of Animals) and was outraged at the treatment of animals housed for human consumption. So, at 4 years old, he was designing his own posters and putting them up on posts in the neighbourhood about "saving the chickens". I so admired his intensity and passion to involve himself in causes that were important to him, and for quite a while, part of each of the kids' Christmas presents was an adoption of an animal at the zoo for the year…whether a bear, a wolf, a fox. They felt they were contributing to some animal's welfare, at least and it made them proud.

It was in this spirit that I suggested to Jeff one year that we have a Petland party for David's birthday. One of our favourite (the kids and me) things to do some evenings was to go to the nearby pet store and visit the animals. David had become fascinated with reptiles and I struggled to get Jeff on-board with having one. I researched out a creature…an African, vegetarian spiny-tailed lizard, that I promised him I would help David take care of and wouldn't require any worms, crickets, mice or bugs to feed. Finally, Jeff relented, and at the end of the party when the party lady left, after bringing in a multitude of pets for the kids to learn about and hold, she left behind the lizard. David was frantic, worried that she had forgotten the poor little creature but when Jeff and I showed him Xera's (the name David chose for her) new terrarium, he was overjoyed. He spent hours researching out her origins, how to care for her and playing with the little creature, who had an adorable little turtle-face and was very shy and gentle.

From a young age, David, like his sister later, loved baking and cooking with me. I had decided early on that even if things took much, much longer to make with kids' help, it was worth the pleasure of the time with them and their pride at what they had made. They learned about arithmetic in baking and cooking recipe measurements, and David, in particular, showed a keen interest in trying out new things, substituting ingredients. He loved walking up the spice aisle with me at the grocery store, stopping to inhale and try to identify the smells of spices as we passed. Although he was not a "veggie kid", he adored all types of exotic fruits and instead of a "cookie credit card" at the local grocery store, he was thrilled to get a taste of all sorts of tropical fruits that the produce guys would cut up for him to taste.

Like I said, David was definitely his own person...very individual, hard to classify. He had so many passions, things that engaged his interest, but because many things came to him so easily, he was prone to give up when it took a lot of work to "get it"...like guitar, like multiplication tables. Try as I might, I found a "multiplication rap" music tape that I would dance around with him to sing along. I made up laminated exercise sheets all the way up to the 14-times, but all that resulted in was tears, his hands slamming on the table out of frustration and Jeff saying not to bother him about it anymore. David was a kind of kid who needed to do things in his own time, like in swim classes he staunchly refused to dive off the side of the pool for 8 out the first 10 classes but one day, sitting on the side of the pool, he made up his mind to do it and quietly dove in. He seemed to need to talk himself into things sometimes and I learned to just let him ease himself into things.

Parents loved David because he was respectful and interactive with adults. When they didn't know what was going on at school, they would call me because they knew that David always talked to me about what was happening there. Other kids would say that "nothing" had happened in their days, but David always had a steady supply of anecdotes from his day. But he was beginning to share less and less, retreating to his solitude and I was getting worried…

Chapter 5: Jackie

My darling Jackie was born almost 3 years after David. Again, the biggest baby in the nursery at 8 ½ pounds, her dark blue eyes (soon to turn dark brown) and reddish-brown hair framed a darling little face that gazed up at me so trustingly. David had been thrilled with his little sister, chatting constantly to me while I was pregnant about what he was going to play with her, what he was going to help feed her, what they would do together. Even before my in-laws had a chance to hold her, David proudly (with arms nearby, just in case) held Jackie on his lap and cooed to her gently. They drove each other crazy as they grew, but there was always a huge bond of love between them and both staunchly defended each other in any situation. What more could a mother want?

I can hardly remember when Jackie wasn't singing and talking. Like David, she seemed fascinated by everything. Animals, sounds, music, any activity piqued her interest. She adored going for walks in her snugglee with David and me outside. He taught her, along with me, how to catch and throw a ball, how to climb, run, count and read. Like him, she learned everything so quickly. When it came time to learn to ride her bike, he ran to kiss her tears when she slowly rode right into a tree in the park on her first solo jaunt.

Jackie beguiled everyone who met her. While David had been a little joker, enthralling people with his made-up jokes, stand-up comedy and stories, Jackie was a more serious child. She, too, had an intensity about her in everything she tried. At 5 years of age, she wanted to audition for the Girls' Choir and the choir-mistress was entranced by her…"perfect pitch!", she exclaimed and enlisted her in the program for girls several years older than her. Jackie quickly showed her talent for memorizing music and soon was singing in any language they could throw at her. I began her in private singing lessons and she wanted to learn piano, so I found a teacher who would come to the house to give her lessons. But Jackie's ability to memorize the music from reading it once (which seemed to have skipped a generation, coming from my Dad), drove her teacher to distraction trying to get her to go back and look at the specifics of the music. Like David, she was not thrilled with the concept of practicing. Nevertheless, she gamely competed and did well in music festivals in voice, musical theatre and piano as well as taking her Music Board exams.

When she became bored with the choir, Jackie wanted to join a program that included dance choreography as well as singing and went on to join the Youth Singers. There, she found her nirvana with other kids who lived and breathed music and performance. For many years, I volunteered long hours and David would bring his homework to her long and numerous practices. She worked her way up to solos that left people breathless with the maturity and emotion she would project into each song.

Having learned how to throw and catch early with her older brother, Jackie wanted to join a baseball team and she resolved to join a boys' team because they "threw better and weren't afraid of the ball!", she proclaimed. She became a team favourite and played with them for as long as they'd allow girls, then switched to soccer to be like her big brother. Although it wasn't her best sport, she was again a team favourite and always played her heart out, the best she could. From her summer camps, Jackie had shown herself (like her father) to be very coordinated in racquet sports. Along with David on Sundays, we'd play badminton, squash or racquetball, whatever courts were available, and she ended up winning the Silver Medal for the City in badminton at her age level in junior high school.

Like David, Jackie took Tae kwon do with me in family classes. Unlike David, she didn't enjoy the sparring side of it, much preferring the patterns and socializing. I have to give her credit though, she made it up to her red belt before calling it quits, although I was still heart-broken. A highlight for her was singing the National Anthem at one of our city tournaments and there wasn't a dry eye in the house.

Jackie loved horses and she, David and I would go riding at the stables in the urban park near our house. She decided she wanted to volunteer there to look after the horses and ponies, so she spent many a weekend brushing them and cleaning their stalls for them in return for free rides. Drama was a passion for her and David dutifully took drama camps with her sometimes during the school year and summer holidays. She could sure put on a show!

School was an easy transition for Jackie, as she had begun at play-school and pre-school and learned to read early, like David before age 4. She easily mastered languages in school and did very well academically from an early age. Teachers and parents loved her, and she was the champion of the under-dog. Jackie seemed drawn to the sad, lonely, neglected kids who didn't fit in and although this ended up costing her popularity with the in-crowd, she didn't care. I was proud of her tenacity and spirit of caring, but it cost her dearly in her social world at school. She was beloved by kids and parents in all of her extra-curricular activities and I nurtured and encouraged those friendships strongly, to help maintain her social self-esteem.

Jackie started a diary from an early age, before age 7, writing about her feelings, her friends and her experiences and we used to joke about where she kept the key to it. Although I had started one when I was young, I never seemed to have much to say and yet Jackie always seemed to enjoy the chance to express herself. Her teachers loved the imagination in her writing and she could spin an amazing yarn, either in writing or verbal story-telling from an early age.

Like her older brother, Jackie looked forward to our lunches together once a week. We would catch up and chat about everything that was going on in her world. She loved eating foods from all cultures and nationalities but unlike David, didn't seem as interested in learning to cook them. Jackie was fascinated with different countries and cultures, though, and was an avid reader who the librarian in her school would save books for every day as she read almost constantly in any spare time. Travel was as exciting for Jackie as David from an early age and they loved our trips to everywhere. One of the best parts for them was that I would fill their travel back-packs with new games, toys, disposable cameras and snacks that I wouldn't let them open until we were on the plane and I must say, they were never bored on any flights!

Jackie's hair grew in long and blond and she loved it at night when I would sit on her bed and French-braid it or wrap it in hair-rags to create curls. Sometimes, we'd put in coloured beads in side braids in the mornings when there was time. Those times together were precious to me with her. Her dentist suggested that she needed braces on her teeth when she was about 9 and I dutifully took her to 3 orthodontists who each gave a different course of treatment: one wanted to remove her eye teeth to make room for the rest, another wanted to shave down several of the teeth, but a third suggested some time with spacers (much less intrusive) and when they were ready, a set of braces for her upper teeth for a couple of years. Jeff said he'd go along with whatever I chose, and I chose the least intrusive. It was up to me to get her to all of her appointments with the orthodontist, to deal with her fears, the discomfort and frustrations, but I made it a special time for us, treating her to a lunch at a nearby bagel shop after appointments. Jeff never did meet the orthodontist, nor did he meet the dermatologist who I took her to for a year to treat the painful warts on her fingers that drove her to distraction, hiding her fingers from people. At the end of it all, I treated her to a manicure for her lovely hands that finally had smooth skin and nails.

Jackie's emotional intensity and theatrical abilities seemed to make the pre-teen years with her all the more challenging emotionally (for me at least). Once she hit about 9 years old, it was as if a switch had turned on and she and I argued almost constantly. Everything seemed to trigger an argument between her and me. While every parent and teacher complimented her respectfulness and maturity, and one word of (distracted) caution or admonition from her father would bring her almost to tears, to say that we butted heads would be mild. When we disagreed and she went to her father, he would invariably champion her cause and I'd be the bad guy without him and I even talking about whatever it was. I don't know, maybe it began with my mother-in-law arguing with me about disciplining the kids and Jackie remembered. Somehow Jackie loved me fiercely for what I did for and with her, yet had little or no respect for any expectations I had of her that she felt were unreasonable. It was a pattern that was to repeat itself almost constantly in her teen years…

Chapter 6: D-Day

I was living in hell, the kids were miserable and our home was a cold and brittle place. Little laughter was heard there anymore. The kids would retreat to their video-games and the computer when they got home from school and there was silence at the family dinner table. No one had anything they wanted to share of their day. I struggled to keep some conversation going, asking them about their new friends, figuring I could somehow get in touch with the new worlds they were creating in their lives apart from the family. They quit their various sports and activities and wouldn't join any school sports or clubs, "lame", they called them…"only losers joined" and they didn't want to be losers anymore.

I had had enough and resolved to try one more time. I wrote Jeff another note to get us into some couple therapy to try working on things, and left it for him by his tea one morning. He didn't say anything or write back and the next weekend, waking early on a Saturday morning, I found him making a pot of tea in the kitchen. I closed the door so the kids wouldn't hear us and asked him if he had anything to say about the letter. He replied that he had been busy and from his perspective, he was "working on himself right now". Stunned, I asked him if he didn't want to talk about it with me and he said he had been talking "to a friend about us". When I asked who it was, he said it was Julia. He had been going to her house and talking about our life, our marriage, everything he should have been talking to me about!!! He didn't want to "work on things".

In that instant, it all became so clear to me. He had no intention of fixing our broken marriage, our fragile family. He had moved on, betrayed my trust and broken my heart. I took a deep breath and told him that if he didn't want to make things better, then he needed to move out of our bedroom and into another room. He had already separated us by his emotional distance and lack of caring and we needed to separate to figure things out. He didn't argue, only that he didn't want to move into the basement, maybe into the main-floor office but I didn't want him so close to the kitchen, the hub of the family. I said we needed to tell the kids together and he agreed to do so with me that night.

I will never forget the look on the kids' faces when we told them we were separating but going to try and still live together as a family. David just looked ahead stoically and said nothing. Jackie broke into sobs, looking back and forth from me to Jeff, pleading with us:
"You'll work on it, please?" David rolled his eyes and asked if he could go. Jackie went with Jeff to help him move his things into the basement bedroom. I sat there, frozen in an excruciating moment of time feeling incredibly alone. When I broke the news to Dad over the phone later that night, I told him how sorry I was, that I had tried so hard and I felt ashamed, the first person in the family ever to separate. The warmth of his voice, his gentle words of encouragement reassured me that he didn't blame me and would be there for me through everything. He told me I had always been strong for everyone else and would stay strong through whatever happened. His worries, like mine, were for the kids.

I had to get everything in order and knew I had to see what was happening with our finances. Jeff would still not give me the combination to the safe or show me what was inside. I decided to seek out a lawyer and asked one of our lawyer friends for a referral. She came highly recommended, but in the end cost me much more than she was worth, as she made mistakes that later lawyers had a devil of a time undoing. After my first meeting with her, I told Jeff that night that I was hiring a lawyer. He looked surprised and asked why I "felt it necessary to do that?" I replied that I needed to protect myself, as he had given me no cause to feel safe in any way. He, in turn, hired one of our couple friends as his lawyer, a shark-of-a-woman who kept my parade of lawyers at bay. She was a piranha and cost me thousands of dollars with delay-tactics that left every lawyer fumbling with un-replied letters and phone-calls.

Some of my girl-friends rallied around me while others just never returned my calls anymore. They looked uncomfortable when we would see each other in the neighbourhood or at the grocery store. My one friend who had already been through a tough divorce urged me to get control of and freeze our finances. When I told her I was going to try to sit with Jeff and work through our finances amicably, she told me I was being stupid and would regret it. She was right, but after that she pulled away and our previously close friendship ended. I knew I should have listened to her, but I didn't want to be the bad-guy any more that I already was in the kids' eyes. And it cost me dearly.

In the midst of all this, Dad called me one day to tell me that his doctors had discovered a cancerous growth in one of his kidneys at a routine check-up. I raced to be there for him during his surgery and help his wife take care of him post-recovery. My brother and sister-in-law were there, my brother shattered by Dad's illness. We had always thought he was so strong and now seeing him so fragile and vulnerable, it was hard. Garry and I had become distant over the years through no lack of effort on my part.

After Garry's wedding, he had pulled away and I didn't know why. Dad wouldn't tell me, and neither would Garry when I asked him…he was just really busy with his career. I knew something had happened but didn't know what until he told me while we were there at their wedding years before, Jeff had been a jerk to him and not helped out with the kids. He and his wife, who had originally asked David and Jackie to be their groomsman and junior bridesmaid, reneged on it and decided to not have any kids at the wedding. Their choice, I guess, but it really upset the kids, so I told them that if the kids weren't welcome, I couldn't make it, either. Although they relented, I guess they never did get over it and Jeff was resentful for not being included in the wedding party after Garry had been one of his groomsmen at our wedding…family politics. Would have been nice to know all of this had been brewing for years, but Dad was happy to see us together at his bedside before and after his surgery and while he was recovering.

Hearing of Jeff's and my separation, Garry promised to be there more for me and the kids, but things returned to the way they were when we returned home after Dad had recovered and was back to his old self. The kids missed having their Uncle Garry in their lives and with Jeff's sister and brother out of our lives, we had very little family to reach out to. Alixe was like an Aunty to the kids and I to her son, Nick. My aunt and uncle were starting to deteriorate and as I visited, I saw Uncle start to forget things and to withdraw. He had a stroke and heart-attack one day and I rushed to visit. He did regain his strength somewhat, but was never the same again. My aunt tried valiantly to take care of him in their condo, but it became clear that they needed to move to someplace with more help. She moved them to assisted living and I tried to help as best I could from afar and visiting as often as possible. Dad would worry about Uncle, but he and Uncle never did see each other again after my aunt had banished Dad from their lives for marrying Arlene. After 6 years of looking after him with the help of Home Care, my aunt knew she had to put my beloved uncle into a personal care home. He had begun to wander and have spells of confusion and extreme anxiety. He was diagnosed with an inoperable brain tumour and Alzheimer's and I drove to Winnipeg to help move my aunt to another seniors' residence.

My aunt is not a person who makes friends easily or keeps them. She mostly dislikes people intensely and has managed to make enemies everywhere they had lived. They had moved houses 3 times, each new neighbourhood becoming toxic from my aunt's invasiveness and caustic temperament. They had lived in 3 condo/apartments afterwards with the same results. My quiet, gentle uncle just let things happen and didn't argue when she said it was time to move again. He knew better than to start an argument and he lived his life on egg-shells, really only happy when he was in his garden, but he lost even that as they moved from one high-rise to another.

So again, I struggled to help my aunt make new friends in this new place. It was a new building, as she never liked to use a washroom that anyone had ever used, and insisted on a new-build. They seemed nice enough and there were lots of activities, but she chose not to take part, saying she was too busy visiting my uncle daily. Even at meal-time in the lovely communal restaurant, my aunt went out-of-her-way to complain about water-stains on the cutlery, the portion sizes (they were too big for her appetite, she insisted), the "cliques" she saw at the other tables. As nosy as she was about other people's lives, she considered the rest of them to be "busy-bodies" and she set about to contaminate any relationships that could have formed in her hew home. She provided little support for me, either, as she blamed me for my separation, saying that couples were too quick to split now, and that people just used to stick it out in years past, that I was ruining my kids' lives. Great family support, lots of love there…but more about her later…

When Jeff started staying out nights, I asked him to come outside and talk to me one night that he was still home. I asked him where he was…"at Julia's," he said with his eyes averted, "just talking". "All night? About us? You don't expect me to believe that, do you?" I fired back. And then it hit me…stupid, stupid, stupid me…they had been having an affair. He denied it, that there had ever been anything physical, but they were "close emotionally". I looked into his eyes and I knew the truth, though and my stomach lurched with the realization. I felt sick, so naïve and incredibly blind. I went back inside and called Alixe. She wasn't surprised, and even told me that one of our assistants, Nadia had gone into work late one night, finding Jeff and Julia alone there, looking guilty and embarrassed. Why hadn't she told me?! She had been afraid to make things even more toxic at work…and I knew that my world was becoming smaller…who could I trust anymore?

I went to the local walk-in clinic the next day to have myself tested for STDs. Let me tell you, it is embarrassing to have to explain that while I had never slept around on my husband, my husband was or had been or probably was. It was humiliating, but thankfully I was clear of anything. I decided to join a local fitness club and David joined with me, which was great because we could work out together. I told Jeff that he owed me, that I was doing something for myself and I was charging the dues to our joint account. He didn't argue. I also decided that after wearing glasses and contact lenses since I was 8 years old, I was finally ready to have laser eye surgery. I had watched through the years as procedures improved and the price had come down but never had felt that I could justify spending the money on myself. I couldn't wear contacts anymore, because my capillaries had encroached on my cornea and glasses were uncomfortable and cumbersome. I made an appointment with a local eye surgeon (the best deal and the first one to bring the procedure into Vancouver), and told Jeff that night that I was getting my eyes lasered. And that I was paying for it out of our joint account because he had always promised me that when the time came, I'd have it done. Now was the time, whether he liked it or not.

The kids came to the surgery with me and one of my old friends drove us there and waited to drive us home afterwards. They got to watch it on the TV screen in the waiting room (there's no blood in the procedure, so they thought it was cool), and I returned home to wake up the next day seeing a whole new world. Everything seemed to be in 3D, more vibrant and beautiful than I had ever seen before. I remembered when I first got contacts at age 16, having saved up for them from my various jobs for years, how amazing and real things looked out from behind my glasses. Being able to wake up and see without reaching for glasses, to swim without banging into people (I couldn't wear my contacts swimming, after losing numerous pairs trying, they just didn't seem to stick to my eyes), to see everything so clearly was a dream-come-true. I could literally see the world through clear eyes now.

Although I was growing and figuring things out on my own, it was becoming very hard to keep things civil at home. The tension, even with Jeff and me in separate bedrooms, was as much, if maybe even more intense than before the split. I knew I had to do something about it. He wouldn't move out of the house, as he said we had agreed to try and live together as a "family" for the kids, but I just knew I couldn't stand it any longer. I felt like I was going to explode, the tension was so palpable. I started checking out homes and town-houses in areas close to home from the newspaper. I knew I couldn't afford anything as big, nor did I have the down-payment for one. When I talked to Dad about it, he said he was "lending" me $50,000 for the down-payment and I could pay him back later. I was so relieved and hadn't even been asking for his help, was just trying to figure out with him what to do.

I brought the kids out with the real estate agent and we eventually found a really cute town-house within a 5-minute drive of the family home. It had 5 levels and a single garage underneath: the bottom level was an unfinished basement, the next level up was the entrance off the garage with a powder-room, up the stairs was the open living-room/dining-room/kitchen, up another set of stairs was a jack-and-jill bathroom with 2 bedrooms, another level up was a loft balcony overlooking the main floor and then another set of stairs attached to the wall was a low-ceilinged cubby perfect for the kids to spend time with their friends if they wanted. Jackie would have the bedroom beside mine and David was okay to use the loft as a bedroom until I could get the basement finished for him with his own bathroom.

The kids were excited, and I began packing a few boxes a night at the house. Jeff said "lucky to have a parent to lend you some money", his only response to me telling him I was moving out in a couple of months. Now I've always tried to be a fair and honest person and I set about equitably separating any of his family heirlooms from mine, even though I had been the one taking care of them all our time together. He tried to peek into my boxes one time and I glared at him, telling him he should know better, since I had never cheated him. He guiltily backed away and never did again.

We decided to go through the house and divide up furniture and other possessions we had accumulated before my moving day half-way through December. With notebook and pen, it was amazing to so dispassionately break down what we had bought together into a "his" and "hers" list. When Jeff argued that I didn't get to keep both of the paintings he had bought as presents for me ("half-and half-, right?" he said), I have to admit that I took a perverse pleasure in arguing for the big-screen television, although I was not a big TV-watcher. He could keep the kids' bedroom furniture, I was buying them new stuff as a local store was having a buy-now-pay-later deal, with each getting a TV for their room included.

Moving day couldn't come soon enough for me. I was packed and had emotionally withdrawn from our home of 8 years. Jeff didn't want to be bothered with Jack and I was thrilled to have my little fur baby live with me full-time. I knew the move and strange newness would be tough on the little guy, as especially, like me, not seeing the kids every day. We had decided that a 50/50 schedule with the kids was best for them. They seemed happy with it, and although I knew Jeff hadn't been a very involved parent (to say the least), I figured maybe it would give the kids a chance to have more of a relationship with him. It was a hard decision, because the only times I had ever been away from the kids were when I took care of Dad after his surgery and one conference I went to away from home. All of our holidays had been family ones, I had never wanted to "holiday" without enjoying myself with the kids.

Now the time had come, and the moving van was there. The kids looked flushed with excitement but also wary of changes ahead. They wanted to help and stayed over that first night, our first "sleepover" before they returned to the other house the next morning. We had ordered in pizza and I worked feverishly to get everything out of boxes for the house to look like a home.

Exhausted, I slowly climbed up to bed at 3 in the morning and found both kids and Jack snuggled in my bed, fast asleep. They looked so peaceful and trusting and yet I knew that there were going to be some tough times as we negotiated the new waters ahead. After a fitful few hours of sleep, I awoke to find David helping Jackie set up her room. Bless him, he was helping her figure out where her pictures and posters would go on the walls and she was excitedly flourishing her arms in her new domain. I told him how much I appreciated his help and that I would get to the renovations on his room as soon as possible. "No problem", he said, as his temporary new place on the mezzanine was where the computer was now located, so he had unlimited access to it whenever he wanted.

After making the kids' favorite breakfast of egg-and-veggie burritos and hash browns, it was time to drive them back to the other house. Jack wagged his tail anxiously as we left for the 5-minute drive and I assured him I'd be back-in-a-flash. He settled down by the door, head in his paws with a sigh as he watched the kids and me leave. I knew this was going to be tough for him...he had rarely been without them and I remembered the day we had gone to pick up our new little family member 5 years before...

Jeff had allergies to everything, it seemed and there wasn't a day that went by without the kids asking when they could have a puppy. One day, he told me that a client of his had a litter of Jack Russell puppies - relatively hypo-allergenic, and he was willing to see if he was okay with them. With the kids at a drama camp, the two of us drove to visit her out in the country. When we arrived there, she brought us to a room in her house filled with squeaking, whimpering puppies rolling around everywhere. One little guy, a brave little soul, waddled his way over to us with his little tail wagging up a storm. We both knew immediately that he was the one, as he happily snuggled, nuzzled and licked both of us lustily.

As the puppies were too young to come home yet, we told the kids that we were going on a road-trip the weekend they were ready to be adopted. As we were driving up the country road, I turned to the kids in the car and told them that our family was adopting a new kid - Jack Russell was his name and they didn't mind, did they? They looked warily at me and each other and we silently drove up to the house where we were greeted by a big, black German Shepherd-cross named Eddie, who exuberantly climbed into the back seat when we opened the doors to go in the house. With the kids laughing uproariously, we rang the doorbell and Joan, Jeff's client answered, ushering us into the puppy-room. They had all grown in the 3 weeks since we'd seen them, and Jack ambled his way over to us excitedly. David and Jackie looked at us questioningly when I told them that Jack was our new family member and they couldn't wait to pick him up and bring him home. He showered them with non-stop puppy kisses and happily settled into Jackie's lap to fall fast asleep on the drive home.

That first night, I brought Jack upstairs and the kids and I had a "sleepover" with the new little guy on the floor with blankets and pillows in David's room. He never whimpered or cried but settled contentedly between the two of them all night. After that, Jeff wanted him on the main-floor and I spent the first week patting him to sleep on his bed on the floor in the kitchen, only to be awakened in the morning by pathetic puppy cries. It took him awhile to adjust, but there was never a morning that Jack wasn't there waiting at the kitchen door with his tail wagging excitedly, his eyes mischievously twinkling and ready for the day ahead. There was never a dull moment with that pup. Jack Russells are notoriously amazing jumpers and every morning as I made breakfast, he would jump a vertical distance twice his height to see what Mum was making for breakfast. It was like a comedy movie as he squeaked on every landing.

As I drove up to the other house, my heart heavy with seeing the kids go, Jackie was chattering about her day ahead. David had his head down and mumbled "see ya," as I waited to see them go in the door. Jeff and I had agreed that these first few days, we'd "play it by ear" as to where the kids stayed overnight, to help them adjust in their own way. Then, we'd start on our 50/50 schedule beginning on Sunday evenings.

I drove slowly back to the townhouse. Jack looked behind me as I came in, expecting to see the kids. He had stayed right where we had left him when we went out the door. "No, boy…it's just you and me today," I told him, and he sniffed his way off after giving me a wet puppy-kiss, exploring his new domain. He had to find his "sun spot", as he always had done at home…right near a window in the house where he would lie in the pool of sunlight, following it from window-to-window as the day wore on. And there it was, by the sliding glass doors to the deck off the kitchen. He let out a contented sigh and plopped down for a nap.

Chapter 7: My Aunt

If anyone exemplifies the craziness of the female side of my family, it's my aunt. She and her husband (my uncle) were my god-parents and as tough as life was growing up at home with my mother, the thought of living with my aunt was enough to make me take whatever she could dish out. Mom's sister (her only sibling) was born a handful…picky, wilful, stubborn, a (self-professed) "sissy", who didn't like the outdoors, anything sporting or energetic, dependent (she, like my mother never learned to drive, preferring to be chauffeured everywhere by my uncle or take the bus), critical and negative. She never did live apart from my grandparents, building a home with my uncle (who adored my grandparents and was in turn, like my Dad, treated like a beloved son by them) right next door to my grandparents.

Aunty decided (upon graduating from high school) that she didn't want to go to college (like my mother), although my grandparents had scrimped and saved through the years to be able to send them both. She didn't like blood (so wouldn't be a nurse), didn't like children (so wouldn't be a teacher), never much liked sewing (so wouldn't take home economics), so she decided to be a secretary. She steadfastly maintained that women "in her era" didn't have any other choices and as the years went by, I began to argue that point with her, citing the cases of first women doctors in the late 1800's, first female lawyers and judges in Canada in the early-to-mid 1900's. She just didn't want to leave home, except for holidays.

Her story is that once she and my uncle met when he returned from the War (they met and discovered their mutual love of reading and literature), he told her it was okay to quit work and stay home to wait for him, if she wanted to. I don't think he could take the misery of her complaints about everyone and everything at her workplace. With my grandparents next door, my grandmother (a terrific cook of any type of food despite being unable to read any cookbooks, all she had to do was taste something and be able to recreate it) would frequently feed my uncle. Boy, did he gain weight with my Grandma's cooking! My aunt, in the meantime, began her obsessive-compulsive cleaning regime that made it almost impossible to visit her house without being given slippers, a food-tray to catch any crumbs, plastic containers with any number of interesting treats she had found on sale and lots of napkins.

Her "spare time" was spent reading and watching everything and everyone in the neighborhood from her windows. She didn't care for the outdoors (bugs, flies she was terrified of touching her "they sit on dog poo and garbage!") and perhaps that's where my uncle discovered his love of gardening, his roses, his tools and projects in the garage out back. He was always ready to help anyone with any repairs or work around the house.

I can't tell you how often my aunt called the police on the neighbours' kids who would dare to play on their boulevard (she didn't get that that land belonged to the city, not her). She disliked all the neighbours and seemed to know everything about their lives and I think some of the reason for my adoring grandfather's ulcer and later heart problems was internalizing the stress and turmoil she created in life. Although he was a quiet, gentle man who rarely spoke other than to tell me stories because I voraciously asked about his earlier life, you couldn't help but get stressed out from conversations with my aunt. Like my grandfather, my uncle was quiet and hard-working, but was very well-read. Don't get me wrong, Grandpa was a smart man, but he had to start work at a very young age when he came to Canada as a young man and never had time for further schooling.

Uncle had studied and adored geology on a GI Bill when he returned from the war, but he decided that because at that time, he would have had to work outside of Canada (and my aunt clearly didn't want to leave), he'd switch professions and he became a railway engineer. I am proud to say that Uncle trained the first female railway engineer and was the most egalitarian, humanistic person I have ever known (that, and being a saint for enduring my aunt). He seemed content with doing the long-hauls, keeping him away for over-nights and I don't think he minded it one bit. He did transfer his love of the natural world to me and I learned early on what the names of every rock was that I brought to him. His library of National Geographic, wildlife magazines, political magazines, books and magazines of economics and our mutual love of wildlife shows on television were the magic of my childhood.

When my grandfather required a pace-maker (one of the early ones, the kind that stuck out of the chest like a shelf), my aunt decided that they all needed to move to "make it easier" for my grandparents. So, my aunt and uncle built a house in a nice new area of town with a lake behind them. Uncle set about to create a lovely garden behind it and my grandparents moved into the upstairs so that my aunt could help "take care" of them. It was a disaster from Day One, and my aunt fought constantly with my Grandma. They were supposed to have 2 self-contained suites (that way my Grandma had her own kitchen), but my aunt just couldn't stay away from complaining and criticizing. The neighbors again became a target of her attention and soon, the neighbour kids were egging the side of their house in retaliation.

So, they moved again, this time to a new 50-plus apartment building on a busy street in an older part of town. My grandparents had the apartment across the hall from my grandparents and the misery continued. The one bright light was that my aunt and uncle, who was getting set for an early retirement, (bless him) started to travel and my grandparents were thrilled to be on their own. Sadly, tragedy struck, as soon after my aunt and uncle left for a driving trip in Florida, my grandfather (unbeknownst to us) decided to take a bus to bring us cookies that my Grandma had baked. I got the call at school from my Dad that Grandpa had been in an accident of some sort. He rushed to pick me up at school, then my brother, then home to get my mother (who was thankfully not too drunk yet) and we raced to the emergency room. Wandering around Emergency asking for my Grandpa, we were met by a stony-faced nurse who told us he "was dead on arrival". Needless to say, we were devastated but terrified at the thought of my poor Grandma, who we heard had two burly cops show up at her door and explain to her that her husband was dead.

She was never the same again, understandably. My grandfather had been her whole life, just as she was his...65 years of doing everything together.

It was a nightmare trying to find my aunt and uncle driving around Florida, but eventually the highway patrol pulled them over. I think I've purposely (and perhaps wisely) repressed the reunion when they arrived back home. Someone had to identify my Grandpa's body and my father decided to undertake it to spare the rest of the family. I drove with him to give him support, but he just couldn't do it, he was sobbing so much so I decided to spare him the pain. I don't have to tell you the damage an 18-wheeler will do to someone. Grandpa was almost unrecognizable.

The funeral was something I never wanted to remember. The family decided to have a private viewing (they do that, I don't know why), but it lasted for what felt like an eternity. To this day, I detest the smell of lilies, they remind me of death. My poor Grandma, who had married Grandpa at 16, had to be dragged from his body, as did my aunt. For years thereafter, once I learned how to drive, I would drive Grandma to "visit" Grandpa and have to pick her up from her knees as she begged God to "take her" to be with him. Unfortunately, although I asked my mother to have Grandma come live with us (I'd have given her my room, anything to keep her away from living with my aunt!), she refused, and Grandma moved to a new house with my aunt and uncle. They had built a new house in another neighbourhood, but the dynamics never changed, only got worse.

I have lost count of the times I would drive over to their house with my mother after a screeching phone-call from my aunt with my Grandma sobbing hysterically in the background. My aunt followed her everywhere in the house, gave her no privacy. It was torture for my Grandma to even go to the bathroom, as my aunt would follow her in afterwards and criticize the poor lady for "making smells", among other admonishments. I would invariably arrive to find my aunt and Grandma at the top of the stairs (my aunt always seemed to leave the door unlocked for us to come in), with my aunt and/or Grandma trying to either throw the other or themselves over the balcony. If it wasn't so pathetic, it would have been comical. I'd calm them all down and we'd have some tea, my aunt always promising to leave Grandma alone. But that never seemed to happen, she was incapable of it.

When I left for grad school, my Grandma's health had deteriorated, and she was in hospital until the end. From what I understand, my aunt drove the nurses and nurses' aides insane with complaints about how they addressed my Grandma, how they treated her, how they acted. She went to superiors but to no avail. I reminded her in my calls and letters that as much as she complained, Grandma was the one who couldn't leave and who knew how the staff felt after the theatrics they endured from her altercations with them? (I put it more nicely, of course). In the meantime, with more hatred from the neighbours in their new neighbourhood, my aunt and uncle moved again, to a nice new condominium in quite a posh area (less work, my aunt rationalized, for my uncle not to have to take care of a yard, although I sincerely believe gardening saved his sanity)...

Well, the new place was attached to a religious group, who my aunt acknowledged were "very clean and not pushy with their religion" but she felt it set her apart from them. On my visits back home on holidays, I soon discovered that the "noises from above", of the older gentleman's cane on the floor above them was cause for my aunt to rant and rave and bang her ceiling many times a day. She hated the sound of his toilet flushing as well (don't know how she heard it, but that he apparently did on purpose, as well) and my uncle soon became diabetic and then had a heart attack and stroke one sad night. No one had told me, but he had developed Shingles soon after moving there, no doubt from constant exposure to the stress from which he could no longer escape, having retired and being stuck at home in the condo.

My Uncle never quite recovered. She moved them (again) to a place that provided all meals (albeit in a swanky dining-room), so that she could devote more of her attention to him. I don't know how he managed to survive so long, but his blood pressure went through the roof and I started to see him slip away slowly into another world. She hated the people there, too (there were too many old people, too many "nationalities", too many "cliques") and again history was repeating itself. Visiting there was like being in a fish-bowl, with everyone uncomfortable and warily avoiding my aunt. Uncle silently read his books and magazines, watched whatever television he was allowed to and a conversation I had heard between my mother, my father, my grandfather and uncle came back to me..."who is going to take care of her when we're gone?". Now I understood...

In the midst of this, my mother had died unexpectedly just as we were about to arrive on a visit with the kids back home. As if losing my Grandpa and dealing with my Grandma's death like they had happened yesterday weren't enough, this pushed my aunt further over the edge. Try as he might with his love for Uncle and duty to my grandparents, Dad valiantly did his best driving her and Uncle to where they needed to go even in his own profound grief, but she drove him nuts. The final push happened when he told them of his happiness at getting engaged to Arlene. She unceremoniously screamed at him that he had no-doubt been cheating on my mother (who had been dead for 5 years by this time) and if he ever truly loved her (which she doubted), he should never remarry. That was it. Uncle and Dad would never see each other again, as my aunt wouldn't let Uncle out of her sight.

Dad did go once to see Uncle at the personal care home he ended up in after Alzheimer's and an inoperable brain tumour ravaged his poor mind and body, but Uncle didn't recognize him or anyone by that time. I had tried to figure out a time that my aunt wouldn't be there, but it was hard because she went to visit Uncle every day. Dad called me on his phone sobbing from his car after leaving, devastated and heart-broken at the loss of his "big brother".

I had often wondered why (before there was call-display), my mother would mutter under her breath when she answered the phone and it was my aunt. They were daily calls filled with complaints, misery and often near-hysteria that she would frequently walk away from to do some household chore and return, several minutes later with an "umhm," my aunt never suspecting or skipping a beat. They were so very different, but in some ways so much the same in their negativity, critical nature and dependency. My mother just internalized it and let it out when she was drinking, but it was out there all the time with my aunt. I am amazed that I didn't become a shrink to try and figure out the craziness of my family, but maybe I just didn't want to know...

Chapter 8: Now What?

The night Alixe and I went out had been the weekend before the move. Tony had called me the Tuesday after, in the evening. It had been a surprise, as I hadn't expected to hear from him again. That night had been too perfect, and in my state-of-mind, I wasn't expecting any good surprises. Hearing his voice as I answered, a rush of emotions flowed through me…the only calls I ever got from a man were from Dad or business calls or from girlfriends' husbands, sometimes to talk to Jeff if they couldn't reach him. I felt awkward and he picked up on it. He said he had been thinking a lot about me since that night and how about a date to get to know each other better? Like a deer in headlights, I invited him over to my new place for dinner that Saturday night, the day after I was moving in. Was I crazy? I didn't mention to him the time-line, but panic welled up inside of me. He sounded surprised but pleased and I hurriedly gave him the address to my new place, to come over around 7. I hung up the phone in disbelief…had I just invited him over? I called Alixe and told her and she screamed in excitement but admonished me for inviting him over…"Are you crazy?! You'll be just moved in! What are you going to make for dinner? Let's figure out what you're going to wear!" Oh boy, what had I gotten myself into?

After dropping the kids off and returning home later that morning, I stared at my pantry and decided to make something I had always loved…Cornish Game Hens in a hoisin/sesame/soy sauce with rice, a dish that always came out well. Sweating over the stove, I realized that time had flown, and I had less than half-an-hour to get ready. If Tony was an early arrival, I'd be in trouble!!! With the meal made and keeping warm, I had set the table and ran up the stairs to get in the shower. I had laid out a comfy but stylish outfit on my bed and rushed to get my make-up and hair done before I changed.

Darn my hair, blond, silky and fine, it never went the way I wanted it to. Curling it just resulted in droopy, saggy uneven waves so I quickly put it up with sparkly barrettes around my face. I had never really learned to do make-up properly, as my mother hardly ever wore any. I knew that my green eyes (like hers) were my best feature, so I always underlined them with an aquamarine eye-pencil and coordinated my eye-shadow to complement my outfit…right-or-wrong, that's how I always did it. My lips, thin not full like Jackie's…I could never quite figure out lip-pencil, it always made me look like some 30's screen siren trying too hard. I brushed on some neutral lip-gloss and struggled to get myself into my figure-hugging sweater and coordinating slacks. Just in time, as the door-bell rang (he was on-time!) and I raced down the stairs to find Jack barking at the door. After telling Jack to quiet down, I opened the door and there he was, holding a bottle of wine with a big smile on his face.

Tony was wearing a stylish leather jacket with a beige cashmere scarf casually draped around his neck. I took his jacket to put it in the hall closet and he reached out to give me a welcoming hug. He smelled so warm and masculine and I got a little flustered as I apologized for Jack's rambunctiousness. The little guy was excitedly trying to jump up and say hello, getting his dog-hair on Tony's impeccable black slacks. He bent down and chuckled, tickling Jack behind the ears to which Jack rolled on his back for a tummy-rub. My "guard-dog" was more of a welcome dog and followed us appreciatively as we went upstairs for me to show Tony around.

I quickly explained that I had just moved in the night before and he looked incredulous, but I showed him where all the empty boxes were stashed under the stairs. He looked around surprised at how everything was in its place, but I explained how I had wanted the house to feel complete for the kids when they were over. I asked him to open the wine while I served the dinner and we chatted amiably over the meal. He had never had game hen and complimented my cooking…so far, so good.

Fortified with the wine, I set the dishes in the kitchen sink and we settled into the recliners in the adjoining living-room, where I had the gas fireplace on. A little uncomfortable, I asked if he'd like to see some family pictures and, whether being polite or really interested, I proceeded to bring out my 12 (annotated and indexed) albums of my life before and since the kids had been born. I had always been the one taking the pictures and keeping up with photo albums, so had told Jeff I was taking them, that he could have copies made if he wanted to, but he had shown no interest.

Kneeling beside Tony on the carpet beside his recliner, I showed him the story of my life…from early travels before I met Jeff to our wedding (why was I showing him that?!), to the births of the kids and all of their antics as they had grown. He asked lots of questions and never seemed to tire of my stories. As we worked our way through my albums, I asked him about his family and life. He explained that he was from a family of 6 kids…2 older sisters and one older brother and then two brothers born 8 and 10 years after him. His parents had emigrated from Italy to give the kids educational opportunities when he was only 5. It had been a big adjustment for him, as he didn't speak any English when they had arrived. His older sisters and brother were all married with kids and his mother was angling to get him married. Tony loved all of his nieces and nephews and family gatherings were larger-than-life (I bet!). He loved kids, but hadn't met anyone he wanted to spend the rest of his life with yet, although his mother had been sending his picture back to the old country trying to find him a wife, much to his annoyance and amusement.

So far, so good. We seemed to be getting along okay and he hadn't run after seeing my family history in agonizing detail. He suggested we relax on the rug I had in front of the fireplace and we stretched out with our glasses of wine. We stared into the fire for a little bit and I wondered what to say, what I was supposed to do when he reached over and stroked my hand. It felt like electricity was flowing all through me. I had forgotten how that felt, it had been so many years…as I looked over at him, he leaned over and kissed me slowly, gently. I almost knocked over my wine-glass, slowly pulling away. Gulping, I told him it had been a long time…He murmured "I know" and leaned over to kiss me again. This time, I didn't pull away but let it linger, eyes closed until I opened them and found his eyes locked onto mine.

All those years of missing the physical connection with a man had been simmering and everything from there was a blur. Without even thinking, I stood up slowly, eyes locked on his and held out my hand. Holding hands, I ushered him up the stairs to my bedroom and we slowly made love for the first time. As if in a dream, I fell asleep with my head on his chest to the sound of his heart-beat, the smell of his cologne and the warmth of his arms around me. When I awoke the next morning, Jack was snuggled contentedly on the bed at our feet snoring. I quietly got out of bed and into my robe to let him out and make coffee.

Downstairs, I dazedly looked at the dishes in the sink, our wine-glasses on the fireplace mantel and shook my head in disbelief. Had it all really happened? With Jack back inside from his morning ablutions and noisily crunching though his breakfast, I turned to see Tony peer around the stairs with a grin. He had dressed again and combed his hair, looking almost as fresh as when he arrived and I…well, my hair was all over, I hadn't washed off my make-up yet and I was bundled in my robe with fluffy slippers. He didn't miss a beat though, and thanked me for the coffee I handed to him…2 sugars and a bit of milk, I had remembered from the night before.

Amazingly, it wasn't awkward at all as we sat at the table over our coffee. Tony had this way of making you feel relaxed and comfortable. He explained that he had a family gathering to get to that night, but he'd call me. I rushed to explain that I was leaving later that week for my hometown, driving the kids and me there for the Christmas holidays with my family. He finished his coffee, thanked me for a lovely dinner and evening and kissed me gently before he left after giving Jack a belly-rub. And there it was...he was gone, and I wasn't sure what to think or feel. What I did know was that things had changed for me.

The next week was a blur as I finished up work and prepared for the long drive across 2 provinces (in the middle of a deep-freeze!) to my family. The kids were excited to see their aunt and uncle and we were staying in a suite at their seniors' residence as Dad was down south visiting my brother and his wife for Christmas. Jack was staying back at the other house with the ex- while we were away and looked at us forlornly as we drove off. I felt terrible about it, but there was nothing else I could do, as my aunt despised pets.

Just as I was starting out on the highway on the way out of town, I called my aunt to tell her we were on our way. She worriedly explained to me that a major sudden storm was starting to sweep across the prairies and sure enough, just as I cleared the city, the wind hit us...luckily my wiper blades were new and I'd filled up the washer solution, because snow was blowing at us from straight ahead. Traffic on the highway had slowed to 30 to 40 from 110 and I couldn't even see the lines between the lanes. I followed the one lane that most cars seemed to have gone through and crept along at 30 to 40 kilometres an hour, smoking feverishly.

The trip normally took me about 13 ½ half with bathroom breaks, but I didn't get to Calgary for over 16 hours. My nerves were shot, and the kids were asleep as I filled up the tank, hoping the roads would be maybe even a little better as we continued east. I could barely hear the radio with the storm interference, but knew it was still bad, with few people on the road. About an hour out of Calgary, creeping along at 30, David watched behind us as a huge 18-wheeler barrelled towards us at over 100 kilometres an hour. There was nothing I could do and nowhere to pull off as I saw the driver realize too-late that he was coming up on us fast. He almost clipped our back-end as he wrenched the wheel to the left to avoid us and careened into the median, his load jack-knifing and flipping. I could barely breathe as I saw a truck pull over on the other side to stop and help and I just put my head down to keep going, knuckles white against the steering-wheel.

After over 19 hours of straight driving, I couldn't go on any longer, so with my nerves shot, I pulled off at the closest town where there was a motel and a restaurant, and we got a room for the night. The winds were still blowing snow to cover the road, but I managed to find a parking spot near the motel entrance and luckily, they had a double room. Once in the room, I called my aunt to tell her we were stopping over for the night and would get there sometime mid-day tomorrow. We walked across the snowy street to the nearest Denny's restaurant to settle in for a warm meal. Along with appetizers, I ordered a glass of wine to relax, my nerves still frayed. All I could focus on was getting my aching muscles into a hot bath, then a warm bed to forget this miserable day. The kids chatted amiably and watched TV while I bathed, trying to soothe my aching muscles from the arduous drive. Jackie and I shared the one bed while David took the other. When I awoke to my alarm the next morning (I wanted to start out early and get there already!), it was to even more blowing snow but I just needed to get there so we set out (slowly again) and lumbered our way along, arriving in mid-afternoon, over 30 hours after we had left Vancouver.

My aunt bustled excitedly to greet us and Uncle waved anxiously, standing with his cane as we brought in our luggage. I could see the wariness but then recognition in his eyes as I went over to give him a hug. He stared at the kids in confusion, as they had grown since he had last seen them. I gently introduced them again and he seemed satisfied, bending to receive their gentle hugs and kisses. He had visibly changed a lot since I had last seen him, thinner and more bent, his eyes still warm but vacant at times.

We brought our luggage up to our suite down the hall from their suite, freshened up and went to meet them to go down to the restaurant for dinner. With the kids chattering along the way with Aunty, I followed along more slowly with Uncle as he shuffled along. Wary eyes greeted us at the restaurant and my aunt hustled us to their table near the window. There were no other families there and certainly no children, so all eyes were on us. Aunty did her usual preparations for dinner...inspecting the silverware and putting napkins out to receive hers and Uncle's plates for the meal. She made sure to tell the kindly servers to bring her niece, great-nephew and great-niece "larger portions", as we had "healthy appetites" and she ordered for herself and Uncle. He sat quietly through her ministrations as she chose his meal and juice before dinner for him, then she proceeded to tell me everything about all of her fellow residents. She hated almost all of them and described the "cliques" of bridge-players, bingo-players and "divas" among them. It was an uncomfortable meal of whispered conversations around us as we scoffed down our dinner to get out of there as quickly as possible.

After dinner, we were to go back to Aunty and Uncle's suite for a glass of wine and some pop for Uncle and the kids (his was sugar-free because of his late-onset diabetes). Aunty gossiped on about everyone as we passed by the puzzle and card room on the way to their place, casting withering glances at the residents enjoying themselves playing cards. Jackie and David, both avid puzzle enthusiasts, asked if we could go there afterwards on our way back to our room. I agreed and settled down for a couple of hours of non-stop complaints from Aunty while the kids and Uncle silently watched TV. He still seemed to be trying to figure things out as we said good-night to go back to our suite but happily engulfed the kids in his arms for a hug.

On our way back to our suite, we went to the games-room that also had computer terminals and the kids found themselves a great 3-D puzzle to work on together. I accessed my email account remotely on the computer and was surprised to see an email there from Tony. He said that he hoped we had arrived safely and wished me/us a happy holiday. He went on to say that he had really enjoyed meeting me and our evening together, it had been wonderful company, but he wasn't sure where he wanted to go from here. With the complications and confusion of my life, the divorce, the kids and business with my ex-, he was thinking we should "take it slow" because he was in "uncharted waters". Fair enough, I understood.

While I had been thrilled and surprised to see that he had written to me, my heart sank at what seemed to be his honesty and reticence. What could I expect? My life was in shambles right now and it would take some time to get it back to any sense of normalcy. David noticed my blank stare and asked me what was the matter…what could I tell him? I said it was just something with work and when they were ready, we went back to our room.

Later that night after they were asleep, I went back to the games-room and sent an emailed reply to Tony. I understood how complex my life was and how much simpler he lived his life. I had appreciated and greatly enjoyed our time together and if that was it, I understood. I honestly did. I was neither bitter nor cloying, just speaking plainly from my heart. If he had come to know anything about me, he would know it was honest and true. "No expectations", I told myself as I sent it, expecting that to be it…back to reality.

In bed later that night, I was thankful for having met Tony and awakening a part of me that had been long-dead (or maybe just hibernating). I thought about the work ahead with the kids, trying to make their lives as seamless as possible between 2 homes, about the business, trying to keep things civil between Jeff and myself, and about my future. I had never ever even thought about meeting someone and had resolved to stay single so as not to complicate the kids' lives even more, let alone thinking that anyone would want any part of my raggedy life, my sense of self torn apart and feeling like those puzzle pieces waiting to be put together. I had my work cut out for me and if that was alone, that was fine because that was how I saw it happening from the day Jeff and I had split.

Staying in town for 10 days, we drove Aunty and Uncle on outings to the area mall (the kids patiently sitting with Uncle on a bench as Aunty dragged me along to see the holiday sales), to the old neighbourhood I grew up in, and to the one my mother and aunt had grown up in. I drove her and Uncle to see their first home beside my grand-parents' and around the back, to see the yard Uncle and Grandpa had so lovingly tended. Both new owners had cut down the beautiful crab-apple trees I used to climb, and my grandfather's huge vegetable garden and Uncle's perfect rose-garden had both been paved over for extra parking. I regaled the kids with tales of my childhood there and they listened appreciatively. I appeased my aunt's pre-occupation with death and cemeteries by driving them to "visit" the family graves in both cemeteries…the one that we could park close to, but I had to tamp down the snow to make a pathway for Aunty to be ushered along, and the older one that she kept forgetting where everyone was buried and the kids and I trundled miserably through huge piles of snow to try and find them. We couldn't find the graves there and I never heard the end of that one with Aunty. All the while, Uncle sat stoically, quietly staring out the window, lost in his own thoughts and memories. I never did manage to get any time alone with him while we were there, as Aunty watched his every move and seemed to follow him everywhere. He seemed oblivious to it or had resigned himself to it and spent his time reading or watching TV, sometimes watching the kids, fascinated as if it was all new to him.

The day came for us to leave and Aunty tearfully loaded us up with frozen bags and bags of "goodies" she had brought up from the dining-room and kept in the freezer. The kids dutifully thanked Aunty warmly and gave her and Uncle huge hugs and kisses as we got into the van. I did the same and watched sadly from the rear-view mirror as Aunty ushered Uncle back inside. He looked so frail and tired, not the robust, jovial jokester who teased me mercilessly with a twinkle in his eyes all through my childhood.

I adored that man, always ready for a game of chess (he taught me and had built a chess table for me as a Christmas present one year), a tromp in the snow (he used to help me build snow-castles and snow-tunnels and forts in their backyard when I visited), a discussion about politics or wild-life (he was an avid reader, receiving more economic, wildlife, political and geographical magazines than even some libraries), or teaching me to use his tools and whittle in the garage behind their house. My love of gardening came from Uncle, as I followed him from rose to rose sniffing and admiring the beauty and delicacy of the gorgeous garden he created. Returning from the war after enlisting under-age, he seemed to enjoy the peace and solitude he created in his garden, perhaps away from the non-stop chatter and complaints from Aunty.

We arrived home safely from the drive and I dropped the kids off at their father's, picking up a joyful Jack to bring back home with me. I took him for a walk when we arrived and then set about doing the laundry from the kids and me. After dutifully calling Aunty to tell her that we had arrived safely and had enjoyed her treats along the way, I settled down for the night to get my head ready for work the next day. Dad had arrived back home from visiting Garry and his wife and called to tell me he was home. He asked about how Uncle was and was saddened to hear of how he had deteriorated, but felt powerless to do anything about it or see him. He asked about the kids, if anything else was new and how I was settling in…how was "that darn dog" (he loved Jack and the feelings were mutual, as Dad's father, my grandfather in England had raised Jack Russells and seemed to have an affinity for all animals). He asked about how I was settling into the new place, how the business and the divorce were going (his hatred for Jeff had only increased with revelations about his infidelity) and how the kids were doing in school.

After filling Dad in on everything, I hesitated and then told him I had met someone, maybe…he was silent for a moment and then asked about him. I told him how I had met Tony ("Good for Alixe, I knew she'd get you out-and-about!" he chuckled). Dad reassured me that he was glad I was getting on with life, as he had only ever wanted me to be happy….had I told the kids yet? I told him that until I knew where things were going, I wasn't going to get them involved and he agreed that was prudent. After sending each other much love and wishing a good night, I got off the phone to get myself ready for work the next day.

Chapter 9: Back to Reality

I arrived early for work the next day to my usual busy schedule. On a break away from clients, I called my new lawyer (a fellow who had a practice in our building) for any word on progress. His big voice booming, he swore loudly about how Jeff's lawyer wasn't returning any calls or replying to his letters to get on with things. I had switched lawyers from the one my friends had recommended, as it had become clear that she wasn't doing me any good. It even turned out that she had mistakenly forgotten to have dower releases signed by Jeff and me, so when I moved into my townhouse, he had put a lien on my property.

At my last meeting with her downtown (I hate driving in downtown Vancouver and rarely go there), I had left my van parked for too long at a meter on the street (apparently they tow after 5 pm, who knew?!) and came downstairs to find it gone. Calling the city at the number listed on the meter, I was sure that it had been stolen but found it had been towed to an impound lot, with my winter coat inside. It was a day when I was to take David to his therapist's appointment (I had insisted that the kids both speak to someone to help them deal with things). I quickly called his school to tell him to take a cab to the appointment and I'd pay and meet him there.

Struggling along Vancouver's snow-lined streets, frozen without a coat and the wind blowing me mercilessly, I tried to race to the appointment but managed to fall on a street-corner, my divorce papers sprawled all over beside me. I was almost in tears as I arrived to find David beside the taxi as he waited miserably for me. He hadn't wanted to talk to anyone and really resented having to go, but I quickly paid the driver and walked inside with him to meet the therapist. She was friendly, kind of "new-age", and I sat in the waiting-room for the session to finish.

After paying for the session and calling for another cab home, David sullenly sat beside me in the back seat, refusing to say anything. When we got home without the van, Jackie asked what had happened and I told her, to Jeff's obvious amusement as he was there making dinner for Jackie. He refused to drive me to pick up the can, so I took another taxi (after finding an old coat to wear) to find the van and get it out of impound. Wandering around that lot in the cold after paying almost $200 in fines and for "storage", I had rarely felt so miserable and alone.

After the fiasco with my first lawyer, I had resolved to find a new, good-ol'-boy, a guy who (maybe) understood men better. I had spoken to Bob in the elevator a few times and while getting coffee at the coffee-shop downstairs and he seemed to "get it", I made an appointment with him and he seemed eager to get things done for me. Finally! But here we were going again…although Bob was very honest about not over-charging or jacking up his fees, it was taking his time and frustration to continue things along with Barb, Jeff's lawyer, who I was sure was laughing all-the-way-to-the-bank. I told Bob that I was going to try to settle some things with Jeff myself and he drawled incredulously that Jeff was already showing his true colours with the lien on the property and the game-playing via his lawyer. I told him to keep trying from his end and I'd think about what I might try to propose.

After a busy afternoon while I was putting things away to pick up the kids from school, I checked the voice-mail on my cell-phone. There was a message from Tony, much to my surprise. I didn't have time to listen to it until later that night after I had taken the kids to their activities and dropped them off at their father's for the night. Taking Jack for his evening walk, I listened to Tony's calming voice as he asked me to call him. Jack and I ate dinner together (he really was a noisy eater, but insisted on waiting to eat until I sat down to eat myself, the little gentleman!) and after doing the dishes and calling the kids to say good-night (we had agreed on before-bed tuck-in phone-calls before I had moved to my own place), I took a deep breath and called Tony back.

Tony immediately apologized for not calling sooner, but he had lost my business card and by some miracle, an old friend had been the guy who had installed my new house phone. He had called him to plead his case and asked him for it and I guess the guy had finally given in. We caught up on things since we had last met before Christmas and Tony regaled me with tales of all the family gatherings. We talked for hours and he asked me to go out for dinner the next Friday to a new chic restaurant his friend had opened. He was to pick me up after 6, to give me time to get ready after work...what was the appropriate dress for the restaurant, I asked in a bit of a panic.

I had rarely been out to anything fancy in years and Tony reassured me that I had plenty of outfits he had noticed in my wardrobe that I would look great in. He had paid particular attention to my wardrobe as we had toured my town-house and had commented on my "interesting" collection. Okay, I had a hard time letting things go and still had an amalgamation of my mother's, my ex-'s aunt's clothes, some of my aunt's cast-offs and my grandmother's shoes that I hadn't been able to part with, much to Alixe's frustration. She always laughed at my inability to let them go but I always protested that they were still wearable and too good to give away.

The week raced by, Jeff cold and unresponsive at work and our employees wary, enduring the increasingly strained dynamics there. I knew that the youngest, a bright, vivacious young woman, had been anxiously looking for work elsewhere, as I had seen her quickly change the screen on her computer from the want-ads when I would come into the office. I had left Jeff a note at his desk on the Wednesday that maybe we could meet to "settle some things on our own" that Sunday over coffee, while the kids were at their drama workshop. He had written a reply that "Okay, let's try it. Let's meet at noon", so maybe I would make some headway.

Friday came, and I struggled to finish off my day, the messages and calls, all the meetings…I always liked to end the week caught up on everything, if possible. I ended up leaving the office late. Alixe warned me to not leave it too late as she left to go home for the weekend and grinned as she told me to call her with the "gory details" after my date. I raced home to let Jack out and feed him with just enough time to shower and get ready before Tony was to pick me up.

I would always lay out my clothes before I showered, but I still had no idea what to wear and panic-stricken, surveyed my motley collection. Sure, I had some good work-clothes, but what to wear to a fancy restaurant? Putting on my make-up hurriedly and pulling my hair up with barrettes (again, had to figure out something new eventually), I decided on a skirt-set I had worn to one of David's evening recitals. It was a lovely teal-green and complemented my eyes, I thought, so I struggled into it just as the door-bell rang. On-time again! Would I never learn? Jack was yelping his greeting at the door as I raced down the stairs.

Tony smiled appreciatively at what I had chosen as he entered to Jack's snuffling greeting. After a gentle belly-rub to Jack's obvious pleasure and a puddle of pee from his excitement as a reward, I turned to get something to wipe it up, but Tony caught my arm with a flourish and enfolded me in a warm hug. He told me how lovely I looked and bent down to stroke Jack's ears as I trotted off to get some paper-towels. Everything cleaned up and Jack happily chomping his way through a new doggie-bone, Tony helped me on with my coat and we drove off in his antiquated ("classic") Mercedes he had bought from his father years ago. As it belched fumes and sputtered along, I saw the neighbours peering through their windows.

I hadn't realized it was a more senior townhouse complex, and it turned out they were not a very friendly bunch. I had already received a "condo-owner's warning" in the mail that I hadn't cleaned up after Jack on one of our nightly walks (although I always did) and they seemed none too pleased when I moved in with teenagers, watching warily out their windows. It seemed like I'd moved into a place filled with Aunties...

Driving along to Tony's country music (why did he have to love the one type of music I despised?!), he chatted about his week and asked about mine. He had a very busy practice and was very discrete and professional, only saying that he was seeing more and more families that were separating. I told him about the meeting I had proposed to Jeff on Sunday and he quietly warned me not to have too high expectations. When we arrived at the restaurant (so beautiful and sophisticated!), we were seated quickly and his friend, the owner came over to visit. He looked at Tony questioningly as he introduced me and suggested several of the nightly specials, as well as Tony's favourite oysters for an appetizer. Now don't get me wrong, I love seafood of every type but raw oysters had never been on my hit-list. When they arrived, Tony encouraged me to try one, which I did to appease him and I left the rest for him to enjoy...which he did with gusto. The chef hovered over us as we tried our main courses and he seemed pleased with our honest responses of delight. We lingered over coffee and again, ended up talking for several hours when Tony realized that the waiters were hovering to try and get us out. As we drove back to my place, Tony mentioned that he'd like to talk for a while still and came in, much to Jack's enthusiasm.

I made a pot of coffee and brought out the Bailey's as we sat by the fire. Tony explained the reasoning behind his email to me when I was away for Christmas. He had been surprised and thrilled with our meeting but began to think about the differences between us...in ages, in relationship status, in me having kids, in how complicated my life was and how simple he kept his own. Yet as much as he had tried to talk himself out of it, he had been drawn to the connection we had made. He couldn't stop thinking about our conversations, about my honesty and who I was in spite of everything else going on around me. I told him about my reticence, too, having been with someone for so long and my fears of a new relationship, of being hurt again. We agreed to continue to get to know each other and take our time...after all, what was the rush? He reached over to stroke my hair, Jack yelping protectively. Tony laughed and kissed me, and I responded as he knew I would...

The next morning, I pulled on my robe and fluffy slippers to make coffee for us, smiling to myself. Where was this going? I didn't know, but I was sure enjoying myself and Tony seemed to be very comfortable with me, too. He came down for coffee and commented on my "Kiss" collection in the bathroom. I had thought nothing of it but realized that having the (still-boxed) heads of all four band-members sitting on the back of the toilet may have been a little odd. Jeff had disdainfully told me to keep them hidden, but I had been thrilled to dust them off and put them on display in my new place. I had a "Kiss" trivet on my night-table beside my bed for my nightly glass of water, too and sighed as I took Tony to see my box (still not on-display) of a stage set-up, complete with figures of the band. He couldn't help but laugh as I told him about how they had been the first concert I had ever attended at age 15 and they had captured my fascination and admiration ever since. Even David was a Kiss fan and so was Garry, my brother, but Jackie had been the hold-out until I had taken both kids to a concert when they were younger. Jeff had reluctantly agreed to go, and I had done up both of the kids in full make-up. They loved the concert, rocking and rolling along with me, in my excitement holding both of them in the stands as we moved to the music. Jeff had just rolled his eyes and sat there looking on, tight-lipped on the drive home. His tastes were more to Barry Manilow and the Beatles (had I really married that man?!), and my music was relegated to when I was driving in the car on my own or with the kids.

I asked Tony what he, a shrink, thought of my musical pre-occupation and he just smiled and said that it was just me expressing myself, but he had never been enamoured of the loud, frenzied sounds of heavy rock music. His favourite concerts so far were Garth Brooks and Shania…and I explained that when I had first moved west, I had been horrified to find most radio stations were country music. I had never really enjoyed it, as I had grown up hearing some of Dad's favourite old-time country music, finding it too twangy and home-spun for my taste.

Tony had to get on with his day and I with mine, so he finished his coffee and was off with a kiss and hug, a pat and belly-rub for Jack. I thanked him for a lovely evening and he was off. Left to my own thoughts, I started to think about my meeting with Jeff the next day, how to make him see what was right and fair but with Tony's warning in the back of my mind...don't expect too much, keep it short, keep it professional and don't get emotional. I did some baking for my week ahead with the kids and went grocery shopping.

Getting home tired and disgruntled (I had "met" people from the kids' previous school and our old neighbourhood while I was at the store, many of whom looked away and a few who openly showed their displeasure at seeing me), I was sure that I was the topic of conversation again back in the old neighbourhood. Whatever, let them gossip. I had never liked most of them and had never wanted or bothered to "fit in" with their vacuous and money-driven life-styles. I had heard that Jeff's goings-on had been seen and talked about long before I knew about them, that I was a topic of derision and laughter. I poured myself a glass of Campari-over-ice and set about putting away my groceries.

After making myself a little dinner and eating with Jack, I took out a 1000-piece puzzle to do on the dining-room table while listening to some of the kids' music CDs. I really quite enjoyed them, which the kids had really gotten a kick out of, as Jeff hated their music and complained whenever they played it. The phone rang, and it was Tony. He had missed talking (already?) and had been thinking about me all day. I told him about my shopping experience and he commiserated with the mean and vindictive nature of some people but said that maybe they were jealous or threatened by me being out on my own now, which I hadn't thought of before. I had been surprised and saddened by the apparent mutiny of many of the people I had seen as friends. He explained that other couples frequently did feel threatened by the dissolution of a marriage close to them, realizing that it could happen to any of them and "out-of-sight, out-of-mind", they preferred to back away. We talked late into the night, as I got ready for bed and kept talking with the phone propped on my pillow. It all felt so natural as we said good-night and he wished me good luck for my meeting the next day.

I awoke with a knot in my stomach. The thought of sitting across from Jeff, untangling the mess of our lives to achieve some resolution was scary. I didn't know what to expect, but arrived early (yes, me early!) to find a more private table at the coffee-shop. He arrived a bit late, armed with a pile of papers. I had thought long and hard about the business, how to separate it from each other. We had sold the lake-house late that summer. It had been a hard decision and the kids were heart-broken, but I could see no way to maintain the debt on both houses and segregate our individual time there. The kids had played outside with their friends while Jeff and I packed up our stuff, filled with memories of better times there as a family with the kids. I told him I thought that he owed me with some of his future earnings for all the help I had given him to finish his MBA and what I had taught him in the business through the years (as I had always ventured into new endeavours and he had eagerly learned along with me to expand his side of the business), and he replied that I should pay him with some of my Aunt and Uncle's will money for having to endure my Aunt. It wasn't going well…with the movers there to bring things back to Vancouver, Jeff took the kids in his car and left me at the house to clean it all by myself, which took me 6 more hours of misery and frustration, surrounded by memories and ghosts of a happier past but always the good-guy, I finished it for the new owners. Hopefully, they would have happier times there.

At our meeting, Jeff looked at me warily and asked me what I was thinking. I told him I wanted to split the business, for him to keep the phone number (or fax number) and me to keep the other. I wanted to separate our practices (he had been developing a reputation for being unscrupulous in the business community). I was happy for him to keep the motorcycle I had bought him if he reimbursed me for it, and the 2 street-worthy motor-bikes and trailer we had bought for the lake-house and our boat would be sold to be split evenly. The family house was already up-for-sale (he wanted to move to a new place, as well), and he asked me to co-sign for a bridge-loan for him to get the funds for a new house. Not checking the amount he was asking for (as I was shocked at the request), little did I realize that he was actually buying a house for himself and the kids and another for Julia and her kids to live in!!! (I didn't find this out until much later in the divorce proceedings, otherwise I would have lost it at that point!)

I flat-out refused to co-sign for anything, citing that he had done nothing to help me along the way, only causing me, along with his shark-of-a-lawyer, more money and irritation at trying to get this done. His brown eyes (I used to think they were warm) hardened and looked back at me, black like a shark. He curtly said that he would see about selling the boat and motorbikes, but "had to think" about the business, because he didn't want to be "inconvenienced". At that, he left with his papers and I sat for a while, feeling my heart slowly return to normal, dripping with sweat underneath my clothes from the anxiety of the encounter. I drove to pick up the kids from their workshop and they were chatty on the ride home.

"How did the meeting with Dad go?" asked David. He surprised me, as I hadn't told them about it...Jeff must have..."Okay, I guess. No yelling at least," I replied jokingly. "No, I mean it. When are you guys going to get this over with? I'm sick and tired of the whole thing and what's with that Julia?" he asked. "What do you mean?" I asked warily. "Dad had us go to her Christmas party with her and her kids before we left to visit Aunty and Uncle." David mumbled. "He did what?" I asked, trying not to sound upset. "Yeah, and before you two sold the lake-house, he brought her and her kids over one weekend when you weren't there. They sent us outside to play with her two kids while they stayed inside with the drapes closed. What's that all about?" Jackie piped in. "Why didn't you tell me about this before?", I asked them, trying not to sound as sick as I felt. "We didn't think much of it at the time, but Dad just told us the other day that he and Julia are dating now and he's lonely on his own," Jackie answered sympathetically.

I tried so hard to control myself, to bite my tongue and almost bit it through. "How do you feel about it?" I asked quietly, and David said he didn't care one way or the other. Jackie was happy to have Julia's kids to play with. I gloomily drove the rest of the way home, back to start another school- and work-week. The kids didn't want to go swimming like we often did on Sundays, so we stayed home and ate dinner while working on the puzzle I had started on the dining-room table, Jack happily lying at the kids feet underneath. After making sure home-work was done (David never seemed to have any!), they went off to bed, David moderately excited that the renovations on the basement bedroom I was having built for him were starting this week.

Sure enough when I wearily climbed into bed after making lunches for the next day, my cell-phone rang. It was Tony…how was I and how had the meeting gone? I told him what had transpired, and Tony commented that it sounded like Jeff was "playing poker", not showing his hand. I told him about what the kids had told me on our drive home and he was silent for a while. "Are you surprised?" he quietly asked. I guess I wasn't, but that Jeff had gotten the kids involved really upset me. He asked me if I had told the kids about him and I said I hadn't yet, waiting until the "right time". He said it would be an interesting first meeting when it happened but agreed neither he nor they were ready yet. He asked me if I'd like to come watch him play basketball with his brothers on their team next Wednesday, as he knew that Jeff and I switched off our weeks with the kids mid-week for an evening with the other parent. His two younger brothers and older brother played on the team and Tony had been a basketball whiz, offered scholarships to university to play.

"Are you really ready for them to meet me?" I asked. "Yes, I've told them all about you and they're looking forward to it, especially the younger ones," he reassured me. "You haven't mentioned me to your parents yet, have you?" I asked shakily. "No, but they'll know soon after you meet my brothers.", Tony replied. "You still have to meet my friends, let me get their opinion of you," he joked. Now that was going to be a nerve-wracking experience when it happened. "And you have to introduce me to your friends, let them tell you what they think," he continued. "Hopefully they won't think I'm after your money, after all I am a relative youngster," Tony teased. Again, we talked until all hours of the morning and my alarm sounded way too early the next day…maybe I was too old for all of this?

Monday passed by and Tuesday was parent-teachers at David's school. Jeff and I had been asked to meet with the principal about his attendance and performance and I was frantic…what had he been doing? Meeting Jeff at the school, we had a chilly reception from the principal and sat down to find out more. Turns out David was leaving for school from his Dad's (near the school) and then going back home after Jeff left for work. He wasn't completing either class-room assignments or homework and I explained that even though I asked him all the time, he never said he had any homework. Jeff said to the principal that he and David were "buddies" and he'd talk to him about it. The principal smiled appreciatively, and I acidly observed that parents aren't supposed to be "buddies" with their kids, they were supposed to be there to guide them. The principal looked uncomfortable, cleared his throat and suggested that we set up a communication book between school and home that would record David's homework and assignments each day, with room for each of us to write responses to the teachers. Great idea and I stuck with it, but Jeff rarely read it (David told me as I admonished him one day for "forgetting it" at school) and never wrote in it, whereas I kept a dialogue ongoing with the teachers. He ended up "losing" the book, but I continued on meeting with his teachers each week, trying to figure out ways together to help motivate David.

I felt like we were losing him. The teachers told me that the kids he was associating with were a "bad crowd", skipping classes and never doing school-work either. They knew David was very bright and full of "potential", so were trying hard to help. I tried to get to know his friends, inviting them over for dinners or sleep-overs, meeting their parents (when any were around when I dropped them off). The one bright spark from this time was David got a part-time job at a pizza joint between both houses, and he was at least motivated to show up there for work.

Wednesday came and the kids were to go to their dad's after school. I got home from work and took Jack for a walk after changing into jeans. After feeding him his meal, I drove off to the community centre where Tony and his brothers were playing. They were all stretching and doing drills when I arrived and Tony waved, motioning me to the bleachers. His younger brothers, Tim and Todd came over to meet me. Todd was tall like Tony, gentle and soft-spoken. He shook my hand politely and asked if I'd be coming out for beers after the game. Tim was younger and more out-going, the shorter of the two and he winked at Tony, said "Pleased to meet ya!", and was off to get ready to play. Tony's older brother Tom looked on, smiled and nodded from the court. This was going to be interesting…

The game was fast-paced. Tony was clearly the leader, yelling orders at his brothers (and his cousin, one of the other team members) and cheering them on at the same time. He scored many of their points and was an assertive (even aggressive?) player, but beautiful to watch as he confidently dribbled around the other team, setting his brothers up for shots. They won handily and did their team cheer, off to the locker room to get changed. Tony, Todd and Tim went to a nearby pub for chicken wings and beers afterwards and I marvelled at the easy, relaxed and loving relationship that was so clearly evident between the brothers. They so obviously looked up to their big brother Tony, and yet each was so individual in his own right. Welcoming like their big brother, I enjoyed myself immensely and was surprised when Todd and Tim asked Tony if I was coming to the championship game the next week. "I don't know, let's ask her.", he turned to me with an eye-brow raised questioningly. "Sure, I'd love to," I replied and both Todd and Tim chimed-in with "Guess you'll meet our parents, then..."

Tim and Todd drove off home after hugging Tony and me and Tony walked me to my van. "They like you, that's pretty clear," Tony observed. "Really, how can you tell?" I asked, thrilled to hear that. "Because they never stayed past the introductions to any of my ex's.", Tony replied. "So how about it, next week, meet the parents?" he asked again, "It'll be easier because they'll just be watching the game and you won't have to talk much.", he encouraged. His older brother had come over after the game to say hello, but from his relative reticence, I was pretty sure I may have my work cut-out for me with the rest of the family...

Chapter 10: Around and Around We Go...

Okay, maybe it was a little too early for them to meet, but David and Jackie were starting to ask questions about when I was going to start dating, "getting out there". I asked Tony over the phone that Thursday night if he was ready to come over for dinner on Saturday night and meet the kids. He took a deep breath and thought about it a moment before replying "Sure, you're meeting my family, why not meet yours?" "Have you told them about me yet?" he asked. "No, was thinking about telling them tomorrow after school over dinner," I told him. "Let me know how it goes. If they're not ready yet, we'll leave it 'til later for me to meet them," Tony answered. He wished me good luck and a good night's sleep before I fell into an exhausted sleep.

After driving the kids to school, I arrived at the office. Jeff had left me a note to say that he wasn't going to give me the phone number or fax number of the business and I was still responsible for half the lease on our office, whether we were one or two businesses there. Alixe was the only brave soul who had stayed working for us, the others having left for other jobs in relief away from the tension of the office. It was only her sense of humour and ability to keep Jeff off-keel that kept things sane there. She did tell me that she saw a storm brewing and that she was starting to look for work, as well and I understood.

In-between appointments, I went to visit Bob, my lawyer, to tell him the non-results of my meeting with Jeff. He "wasn't surprised", he drawled, as he'd faced Jeff in the elevator one morning on the way to the office and it was obvious he was "one cool, shifty customer". "What's with the streak of blond in his hair?" he asked with amusement. "Midlife crisis," I observed, along with the motorcycle, the affair and his new-found friendship for her biker friends. Ugh. My kids were about to be exposed to an element of society I had hoped to protect them from.

After picking the kids up from school, we went to the sports centre to play badminton and then home for dinner. The time had come to tell them and as we ate dinner on top of our partially-finished puzzle, I casually asked the kids if they remembered telling me it was time to start dating? Their heads snapped to attention as I explained to them I had met someone and told them a bit about Tony. Were they ready to meet him, as I could have him over for dinner tomorrow? Jackie nodded enthusiastically. David considered it for a moment and said "Sure, why not?". Jackie continued to ask more questions excitedly while David picked away at his dinner and then took Jack out for a walk. I asked him if he wanted company, but he said he was okay on his own. When he returned, I asked him what he was thinking, and he replied that he was thinking about "how different things are now", how "complicated". I told him if there was any way I could help, just to let me know. He nodded and went up to play on the computer and listen to his music. His basement bedroom suite with its own bathroom was almost done and would be ready next week.
As David really enjoyed cooking, with me and on his own (as I had

heard he was doing much of the cooking for him and Jackie over at their father's), I asked him if he wanted to cook dinner with me. He was quite enthusiastic about it, really, and set about to make a pasta sauce from scratch while Jackie made garlic bread and helped me with salad. I had called Tony late the night before to tell him we were "on" for dinner and he had replied "Okay, here we go!". He knew it was really important that it go well, as the kids were everything to me. I told him that Jack clearly adored him, why shouldn't they and he said "People are more discerning, especially kids and especially when it's their mom." We had talked for awhile but he was clearly anxious about the next day and rang off earlier than our usual telephone call marathons.

True-to-form, Tony arrived on time. Jackie was waiting with me in the kitchen and David was up on the computer. Jack let out his usual yelp-of-joy on seeing Tony at the door and he laughed as the little guy rolled on his back for a belly-rub. Jackie smiled at Tony welcomingly and invited him in as I took his coat. "So far, so good," he whispered under his breath as Jackie lead him up the stairs to the living-room and kitchen. "What smells so good?" Tony asked. "Home-made pasta sauce, salad and garlic bread!" Jackie announced proudly. "You do know I'm Italian, right?" Tony joked with Jackie and she teased him back with "You'll be surprised!".

I called David downstairs from the computer, but Tony motioned that he was happy to meet David on his own terms, at the computer. I led Tony up the stairs to where David sat engrossed on the computer and introduced them. Tony reached out to shake David's hand and they started to talk about computer-stuff. David seemed intrigued that this guy knew so much about computers and followed us downstairs for dinner. With our puzzle still incomplete, the kids and I had put a table-cloth over it on the dining-room table and place-mats over that at each setting. Tony noticed the lumps in the cloth and asked what was underneath. Jackie piped-in that we were working on a puzzle and Tony asked if after dinner, he could help as he loved puzzles, too.

Dinner was a great success. Tony loved the sauce and said it was as good as his mother made. David beamed with pride and Tony told Jackie she had put enough garlic on the bread to give even Jack bad breath, but he loved it! "You can never have enough garlic!" he observed to Jackie, who giggled and agreed. Through dinner, the kids peppered Tony with questions about his family, his business and his life. To his credit, he answered them all honestly and thoughtfully and asked them about themselves, as well. "So, what about you and Mom. Where's that all going?" David asked protectively near the end of dinner. Tony looked at me as he spoke: "Neither of us knows but let me tell you that I think your Mom is an amazing woman and I treasure my time with her." I blushed, and David seemed satisfied with his response "How about working on that puzzle then?" he asked.

We all worked on the puzzle late into the evening, the kids playing their music on the stereo. They seemed so relaxed and comfortable with Tony. We actually finished it together and Tony said it was time for him to go. Jackie seemed disappointed but happy to have met him. David looked him in the eye and shook his hand, saying "nice to meet you" before he went upstairs to the computer. I walked Tony to the door, getting his coat from the closet on the way. I walked him to his car and we kissed good-night, awkward as he was kind of used to staying over. "I'll call you later. I think that went well, I really enjoyed it. They're great kids," he said as he got in his car and drove off home.

Coming back inside, Jackie accosted me with "I like him, he's cool. Maybe he'll teach us some of his Italian cooking another time?"…so far so good. I went off to do the dishes as she climbed upstairs to bed. I told her I'd come up to give her a kiss and hug after I'd done the dishes. David came downstairs to help dry the dishes (he never did that!) as I washed them. "Nice guy. Think he might do some cooking with me?" he asked. "I'll have him back to make dinner with us if you'd like," I answered. "Sure, maybe the next weekend you're here?" I replied. "Sounds like a plan," he said before giving me a hug.

That night, Tony called me late and told me how much he'd enjoyed the evening with the kids. "It's interesting to see you with them. Seeing you as a mother, I can see how important they are to you," he said. "Promise me that you'll tell me if they have any problems with us or me, please?" he asked. I told him they had both given him a "thumbs-up" after he had left and had asked if he could come back and cook dinner with us. He was surprised and thrilled, but still unsure of where things would go, as was I.

Tony called me the next night to remind me that his basketball team was playing in their championship on Wednesday night, would I still like to come? Nervously, I asked if he was sure that his parents would be there. "Yes.", he said, but was quick to add "Don't worry, everyone will be focused on the game." "Okay," I replied, unsure of how it would turn out. As the kids were at their father's on Wednesday night, it would be just me. But when I told the kids that I was going to Tony's game on Wednesday, Jackie asked if she could come. I explained to her that it was her night with her father, but she said she wanted to switch nights, so that she could come. Complications…first, I called Tony to ask how he felt about it. He was pleasantly surprised and said if I was okay with it, he was, too. Then, I called Jeff to tell him that Jackie wanted to switch nights from Wednesday to another night that week. At first, he argued that he had his own plans for evenings but relented when I reminded him that we had promised to play-it-by-ear for what made the kids happy.

So Wednesday came and I picked Jackie up from school. David was going over to his father's after school. Jackie and I stopped for a quick bite on the way over to the community centre. She chattered non-stop, excited to see Tony play and meet his family. When we arrived, there was a huge crowd of family already there. Todd and Tim waved enthusiastically, and I told Jackie who they were. Tony was warming up but came over to hug us both. His older brother waved disinterestedly, and Jackie and I found spots for ourselves to stretch out on the floor. I could feel many eyes on us as we watched the game begin. Looking around, I spotted who I thought his parents were…an older couple surrounded by lots of grandkids. The woman glanced at me and I knew I was right, as her eyes swept to Jackie sitting beside me. She showed no expression on her face but turned back to watching the game. It was quite a game and Tony and his brothers' team won handily. Jackie cheered every time he had the ball and he grinned sheepishly back at me, clearly pleased with her enthusiasm.

Tony's parents left soon after the awarding of the trophies, but Todd and Tim came over to say hello and meet Jackie. She enthralled them, as expected, and congratulated them excitedly, teasing Tony about his ratty uniform. He countered with it was his lucky outfit and grinned appreciatively. After chatting a bit longer, it was time to go, as Tony was driving his brothers back home to their parents'.

Jackie was thoughtful on the drive home. She talked about how great it was for Tony to be part of such a big family, too bad ours was so small. We got home and had dessert together, our ice cream comfort-food and she went off to bed. That night Tony called to say how happy he had been to see Jackie there with me. His brothers had really enjoyed meeting her. He mentioned that his mother had noted she had seen me there "that blond, older woman"…oh boy! She had not reserved judgment but was redoubling her efforts to get him married off to someone from the Old Country. He reassured me that she could keep on trying, but his attention and thoughts were elsewhere. He invited me out with his friends that Sunday night (he knew I had the kids until Sunday afternoon), to watch the football game at a local sports pub. Here goes…now I was meeting the friends!!!

Well, this I knew how to dress for, as I had hosted many a Grey Cup and Super Bowl party at my house through the years…jeans and a sweater should do, not too much make-up and maybe my hair down this time? Tony came to pick me up at home and smiled at my nervousness about meeting his friends. None of his buddies were married, one was in a relationship, but all were "still looking". They had been bugging him to meet me since he hadn't been coming out on the weekends with them since we had begun seeing each other. He said they were anxious to meet this "older woman" who had taken their friend's time away from them.

We got to the bar and there they were, a raucous table of his buddies, ready to run-me-through-the-gears. Did I know about football? Had I played? Who was I cheering for (Winnipeg, of course)? Over the din, I explained that I had gone to a boys' school for high school and had played just about every sport, and was pretty good at most of them. They winked at Tony appreciatively and after I'd ordered my first Guinness, they encouraged me to do some shots with them. No problem, I was from a Russian family (on one side) and could hold my liquor. More Guinesses and shots later, I was raucously into the cheering with them. Seems I'd earned my stripes and other women in the bar looked over enviously. It was a night of good-natured teasing, lots of joking and light-hearted fun and I enjoyed myself immensely. Driving home that night, Tony told me how much his friends liked me…each had pulled him aside and said I was a good sport, when would we get together again? Feeling relieved, I know he was pleased as he squeezed my hand as we drove back to my place.

Having passed the "friends test" on his side, Tony suggested we get together to meet with my friends and it just so happened that one of them was having a "Star Party" (because her husband was into astronomy) the next weekend. Now it was Tony's turn to be a little anxious as we pulled up at Sara's house. Sara's husband Jerry welcomed us at the door and took us out back to where he had his telescopes placed in the yard. I didn't know everyone there, but most of them and Tony got along famously with everyone. It was a relaxing, enjoyable night and Sara pulled me aside to say how much she and Jerry liked Tony already. To see me happy with him and how he treated me so kindly, they said was a treat after watching me agonize through things with Jeff. Neither had liked him very much, nor he them and most of my socializing with them had been on my own.

Alixe was another story…as the most protective of my friends, Tony thought it was a good idea for her to get to know him more. He knew she must have questions (did she ever!!!) and he suggested she come along to another pub night with his friends. Being the most amazing social butterfly, she captivated them all and managed to "have a talk" with Tony outside while I went to the washroom and returned to find them both gone. "Went out for a chat," his friend Derek winked at me as I asked where they'd gone. About half an hour later, Alixe returned with a satisfied grin and Tony came back a bit later, looking maybe a little worse-for-wear.

Back to being her usual the life-of-the-party, Alixe got caught up in the game again and I signalled to Tony to go for a smoke. He readily followed me and told me about how Alixe had grilled him. Her biggest concern was seeing me hurt again, and to ensure that he wasn't "after" my money. He had thought some may have questioned the relationship based on our age-difference and stages of our career, but Alixe had laid it all out. "Probably better to get it out and deal with it," he said, but I think he was maybe a bit surprised at her bluntness. At the end of the night, Alixe gave everyone a big hug before she left, saying to Tony "No hard feelings, eh? Just taking care of my best friend," and he nodded, saying he understood. Alixe had been a big hit with the guys and became a fixture when we would get together with them.

The next week they were over, the kids asked if Tony was coming on the Friday to cook up a meal with us. I told them I had waited until they were back to plan it and they both said they'd been looking forward to it. Their father had "announced" that he was "starting to date" Julia and David told me that he wasn't happy about it, as her kids were "annoying" but there was nothing he could do about it. He seemed pleased that Tony was coming over and we set about trying to figure out what to make. I told them I'd ask Tony over the phone later that night, then we'd shop the next day. When we spoke later that night, Tony was excited that the kids had reminded me and gave me some suggestions about what he'd like to make with the kids.

All seemed to be going well...I was a little nervous with Friday night approaching, but excited at the same time. Tony arrived on time, as usual to Jack's enthusiasm, and Tony and the kids began making dinner. He had brought over some fresh fish and set about making a sauce with David while he supervised Jackie making a vegetable side-dish. Although there was a lot of laughter and fun, both kids really seemed to take to Tony's patient direction and David, in particular, paid close attention to what he was doing. Dinner was a hit and they all "high-fived" each other at their success. Even David was uncharacteristically talkative over dinner. He readily answered Tony's questions about school and his friends, while Jackie chatted along about her life. She even treated us to a song on her violin, much to Tony's appreciation, and after helping with the dishes, they went off on their own to catch up with their computer and calls to friends.

With the dishes done and the kids happily settled, Tony took his glass of wine outside, pensive and quiet. I followed him out on the deck and asked him what he was thinking about. "About where we're going," he replied, taking a sip of his wine. "Look, I'm a pretty simple person and not having a family of my own, I see how involved it is having kids. I work with families and that's one thing, but actually living and experiencing it is another. You really have your work cut out for you and I see how hard you try with the kids. They're still hurting, I can see that. I have to do some thinking about where I fit in, is all." We called it an early night and after checking on the kids, I went to bed early, feeling somewhat anxious and deflated…was he getting cold feet, seeing how complicated my life really was?

As I drifted off into a fitful sleep, my cell-phone rang. It was 2 am…who could be calling? I quickly answered, concerned it might be a family emergency and Tony came on the phone. Had he gotten me up, he asked? No, I was dozing and thinking. "I've been doing a lot of thinking and I couldn't sleep," he began…uh-oh, sounded ominous. "Here's where I'm at," he continued, "I know that it's hard for you getting into a relationship again, learning to trust someone after how badly you've been hurt.". "Mmhm," I replied warily.

"Well, I've never been with someone who has kids and I realized that I had some thinking to do about how I'd fit in, whether I wanted kids of my own, whether we could have kids together. I've had a lot of relationships, but no one I've ever felt as close, as comfortable, as understanding and enjoyable to be with as you. I guess it comes down to this: I'd rather be with you, confusion-and-all, than with any of them. I couldn't think of being with anyone else, with-or-without my own kids. I wanted you to know, because I know it was awkward and confusing how we ended the night. You looked so hurt and wary and I hate to see you that way," Tony explained.

I had listened quietly, surprised at the tenderness and emotion in his voice. I didn't realize he had hit a cross-road. I was just enjoying myself along the way and now it was my turn. "Not that I wasn't thinking about the future, Tony, but you just surprised me with the seriousness of your thoughts. I know that being in a relationship with kids is more complicated, but hopefully more enjoyable…you know my grey hairs I joke about are from being a parent (I teased), but there is a larger perspective when there are kids involved. I'm glad you took the time to step back and I'm frankly thrilled that you can see yourself in the big picture. Everyone seemed to get along so well tonight, David didn't even seem to mind being told what to do! It'll take them time, take us all time to get used to things. I know it's hard for them to see their parents with someone else, it would have been for me."

"No one in my family has ever been separated or divorced, never mind the kids exposed to it," Tony went on, "and it's hard to see any kids hurting. Watching you with them tonight, I saw how much you try to make things okay for them. They're at a tough enough age as it is…" "Some things I can't fix for them," I agreed, "and it hurts so much to see them struggle. I know that sometimes I should be tougher on them but they're already having a tough time and I figure they don't need more grief from me…"

"Love you, Leesa.", Tony said quietly into the phone before we rang off, surprising me with these words for the first time. I surprised myself with how easily I replied the same back, then drifted off into a better night's sleep.

The next day, I had dropped Jackie off at a friend's and David had asked to go to the mall with a friend. As I had some shopping to do there as well, I picked up his buddy (Carl, a kid I wasn't too thrilled with and liked his parents even less). I agreed to meet up with them a few hours later by the mall fountain. About an hour later, I heard my name announced on the loud-speaker throughout the mall, would I please come to the Radio Shack store? Surprised, I hurried over, worried that something had happened to one of the boys. When I arrived there and told the clerk who I was, she signalled for a burly man to meet me. He was the store security guard and he told me that my son and his friend were in the store basement office, as they had been caught shop-lifting. I couldn't believe it, and asked for details. He said he had noticed them looking a little surreptitious as they wandered around the store and then he saw Carl put a CD in his jacket pocket. David had looked about and done the same but had stashed it somewhere else and didn't have anything on him when the guard had stopped them later. He figured David had gotten scared and dropped it behind another pile elsewhere. I asked to see them and asked what they were planning to do, to charge them? I advised him that my son would be rightly punished, and I wouldn't allow him to see Carl again.

When I got downstairs, David had his head down, looking terrified but sullen when he saw me. I asked him what he had done, and he said he hadn't done anything. Confronting him with what the guard had told me, I said that if he didn't admit it, I would advise the store to charge him. Anyway, I wouldn't allow the friendship with Carl to continue on my watch, as he was clearly bad news. He snarled back at me that I was "some mother" who wanted to charge her own kid, he wanted to talk to his father. I dialled his dad and gave him the phone.

When Jeff arrived soon after, he asked the guard and store manager (who had by now arrived, as well as Carl's parents) to not charge them. He smiled at me triumphantly as David leapt up to hug him and when I told him and Carl's parents that I didn't want the boys spending any more time together, Jeff smiled at them and said he had "no problem with it, when can we get the kids together again?". As Jeff left with David in tow, I realized I had lost. In doing the right thing, making David take responsibility for his actions, I became the bad guy and Jeff was the hero, the knight-in-shining-armour. This scenario (me advocating responsibility and Jeff letting them off) was to repeat itself over and over again in the years that followed.

Neither of the children had ever done anything like this...no stolen candies or candy bars from stores like many children have done. I had tried my hardest to teach them responsibility, honesty, and trustworthiness, to help make them good people. I understood that when kids got together, it could embolden them to do what they wouldn't necessarily do on their own, which told me that the friendship between David and Carl was bad news for them both. I felt like I had already lost, as Jeff was even less likely to hold the children accountable than he had ever been.

When I called my Dad after I got home from the mall to tell him (I was so ashamed of David and felt so responsible for what he did), he listened quietly and didn't blame me. He was very disappointed in David, as he knew that he knew better than that, but he put the blame squarely on Jeff's shoulders for how he had handled it. Dad agreed that David deserved consequences for his actions but had instead been rewarded with a "free pass", which gave him the wrong message. We both agreed that it didn't bode well for the future with the kids. Jeff's selfishness, at not being willing to "deal" with things was a familiar scenario but I knew that I couldn't just give in and let the kids get away with things to compete with him. I also knew that there would be even rougher waters ahead.

When I picked Jackie up at her friend's later after dinner there, she was surprised to see that David wasn't with me. I explained to her what had happened, that he was at their dad's and she frowned...I could see those wheels turning and it scared me. We had a quiet night together and when Tony called me that night, I told him what had happened. He was shocked at how Jeff had handled things and compassionate about what I had been through. He knew I hadn't raised them that way, he reassured me, but still I felt so ashamed...

After I dropped Jackie off at her father's the next day (David hadn't called or come back after the debacle the day before and wouldn't return for some weeks), Tony came over for the evening. We talked until early in the morning and as I knew his Mondays started late, I made a pot of coffee and left him a key to my place with a note to have a good day. I had only intended to make it easier for him by leaving the key and had innocently left it there for him, but when I got to the office and off-handedly told Alixe what I had done, she almost choked on her coffee. "You did what?!" she asked. What, I was just being thoughtful, not asking him to move in or anything?! I got on with my busy day and saw a message on my cell-phone during a break from clients. It was Tony and he thanked me for the key, what did I mean by it? Oh boy, now I had opened a can of worms! In my naivety, I had just done what I thought was polite or thoughtful and now everyone thought I was a kook (or trying too hard?)!!!

When I called Tony later that I night, I explained my reasoning behind the key, that it wasn't an open invitation or an attempt by me to entice him. He understood now, he said, but when he had asked a couple of his friends, they had teased him about being a "kept man", that I was "taking things to the next level". My exasperation and clear embarrassment at trying to explain myself made him laugh. So I was a little socially inept in the dating/relationship world…it was "refreshing and honest", he chuckled.

Tony asked me if I'd like to go on a trip with him to Vegas. It would be my first trip without the kids and my first time to Vegas and I really had to think about it. Not that I didn't want to take a trip with him, but I didn't know how the kids would take it. I told him I'd think about it and when Jackie came over the next week (David was still sulking at his father's), I told her about it. She seemed to be okay with it, after a little pout about me "going away" without her. At her suggestion, Tony came over that Friday to spend some time with us, listening to music and playing puzzles, singing along to her music. He was a little off-key, but she was enchanted that he knew the lyrics and he explained that when he had come to Canada with his family, he had learned English by watching TV (mostly cartoons) and listening to music so that he knew the words to almost anything. They really seemed to enjoy each other's company and I couldn't have been happier.

Chapter 11: Spreading My Wings

Our trip was a 4-day junket, staying at the Excalibur. Although I had travelled quite extensively before I was married and had the kids, I hadn't been away for awhile. It was such a freeing experience as we took off for our first trip together. I felt so care-free (the kids were at their father's, David and I had "made up" and I had promised to bring them both back some Vegas memorabilia). I had suggested to Jeff the year before we split that maybe we should go on a trip, "just the two of us", but he had shown no interest (and now I knew why). I had packed my best "going out" clothes and Tony was excited to show me the Vegas he knew. He had spent quite some time there playing in pool tournaments during his university days and seemed to fit in so easily. I, on the other hand, felt a bit like a fish-out-of-water.

Everything was so shiny, so sparkly and glitzy. The only casino I had ever been in was as a volunteer casino worker for our school to raise funds. Now understand that I was far from being a country-bumpkin, having travelled on my own twice to the former Soviet Union in my early twenties as a kind of a pilgrimage to my ancestry, my parents had taken us on numerous holidays to visit with my Dad's family in England, to Bermuda and Hawaii, and I had encouraged Jeff to travel with me and the kids as much as possible…to California, Florida (to visit his family there) a number of times, to Texas and New York twice. I firmly believe that for kids to travel and see the world is the best education you can give them (outside of school), for them to get the bigger picture, appreciate the differences and similarities between countries and cultures.

Vegas was like an adult playground. Night-time was "dress-up" and we saw some terrific shows, while during the day I enthusiastically played the penny-slots as Tony played craps and poker. I watched him a few times, looking so calm-cool-and-collected, expressionless as he coolly surveyed his opponents. He was pretty good at poker and great at reading people. I never strayed from the penny slots, for fear of wasting my money and always seemed to end up even at the end of play, so it was like being entertained for free, I figured. What a great escape from reality it was! I now understood the attraction to the fantasy world of Vegas, albeit a potentially expensive one.

When we got home, I had resolved to take the kids on a trip with me on their next school break. We (their father and I) had promised, after we returned from Disneyland to go there again and stay at a high-end resort there. They were thrilled at the idea, but Tony was not so sure...he felt that holidays were to be earned by kids, in that you took them as a reward. Although we disagreed on this point, he acknowledged that as their parent, I knew what was best and I set about to get Jeff's signed permission for them to go.

For anyone who has been in a messy divorce situation, they would understand that sometimes the expense and legal wrangling you have to do in order to take a trip with the kids away from the other parent is more trouble than it is worth. Jeff made it so complicated and left having the letter written to show to the customs/border agents to the

137

very last minute possible. He was not happy that I was following up on our promise, but I have always believed that a promise made is never to be broken. The kids and I waited with great anticipation for our flight out and Tony said how much he was going to miss me.

When we got there, the hotel (with entrance straight into the park) was amazing and we did everything, rode everything, saw everything there was to see. I had booked in a day tour of Universal Studios and we rode on every ride (even the Tower of Terror, which the kids sent me on first, to see if I would come back alive!!!). We even had a Disney breakfast, which, although David was older, even he loved as the pictures showed his antics with the Disney characters. It was just so nice to be relaxed with the kids, nothing to worry about except the next ride we were trying to get on. It is a memory I will always treasure, those carefree days of fantasy and fun…no homework to argue about, no curfews to enforce, no friends to disagree about.

When we returned home, after dropping the kids off at home with their father, Tony showed up at my place unexpectedly. He had missed me much more than he thought he could, would I like to go for a drive and talk? After I threw a load of laundry in the machine, we drove to the old area I used to live in…an upscale professional neighbourhood that he knew I missed. Casually, as we looked at houses, he mentioned that maybe it was time we should move in together? My jaw dropped…was I hearing right? Although he spent much of the week when the kids were at their father's over at my house, he owned a live-up/rent-down duplex closer to the inner city.

He lived like a bachelor and hadn't even been "ready" for me to see his place for the first month we had been going out. He had apparently spent many nights clearing and cleaning it up and although it was quite stylish and chic, he lived quite a simple, spartan existence compared to my house filled with kid-stuff, family antiques and curios. We spent most of our time at my place when we weren't out, but he hadn't "stayed over" yet when the kids had been home with me.

I guess I shouldn't have been too surprised really, because although we had been seeing each other for 5 months now, after our first month dating, he had whirled me on the dance floor one night and holding me close, proclaimed that I was the "one", the "girl he was going to marry". Even thinking back now, those were giddy times and I don't know if I really believed him. But here he was, with me still trying to finish off this miserable divorce, wanting to live with me and the kids. I was caught off-guard and stared at him with my mouth hanging open, stammering. He looked crest-fallen and looking down he said, "If you're not ready yet, I understand". "No, I mean yes, you just surprised me, is all!" I replied, waking from my reverie. We resolved to start looking for places, but he wanted to meet my family first and we planned a trip with the kids as soon as school was done for the year to visit my brother and his wife in the U.S and my Dad in Winnipeg.

When I called to tell my Dad we were coming to visit, he was very excited to meet this "young man who has captured my daughter's heart and made her happy again". The kids were excited to take a trip with Tony and we drove off down south (after going through the rigmarole to get their father's permission again). The border crossing was "interesting", to say the least. Tony (although he was a permanent resident) still had his Italian citizenship and they asked us to pull over at U.S. Border Patrol. It seems that they needed to do an eye-scan and took him into the back, where the machine wasn't working. Tony, being a computer geek, actually managed to re-install the program for them properly, while I was left to stew out in the waiting-room. Jackie got restless and wanted to go outside, so I said within my sight and to my horror, she started throwing stones out of boredom and by mistake, she hit one of the government vehicles!!! Shrieking and pulling her back inside, she was getting miserable and snarky and I tapped her leg lightly with my foot to remind her to settle down. She responded by yelping loudly that I had hurt her, I had "kicked" her and she began to blubber. David just rolled his eyes and told her to "grow up", but the guards at the counter started looking over at me intently and seemed to be very busy looking at something on their computers. I was petrified, imagining them calling Child Services and having her returned to her father. Just then, Tony strode out from the back offices, laughing with the Border guards, to my great relief and we were "free to go" on our way. It took me awhile to calm down from that one…

When we arrived at my brother and his wife's, they greeted us warmly. The kids were thrilled to see their Aunt and Uncle, who they hadn't seen much of since their wedding many years before. Over drinks, with the kids in bed that night, Garry explained that they hadn't "cared for" Jeff and their feelings about him had kept them away. With the bravado of some wine behind me, I told him that I had missed him and had felt quite lonely and abandoned by him during those tough years. As we made up somewhat awkwardly, Tony watched intently. He had known that I had had a tough time, missing my brother, and he had encouraged me to reconnect. The guys got along famously, and Tony pulled me aside one night to say how refreshing it was to see me so carefree, so joking and goofy with my brother…he had never seen me that way, except with my kids. Garry, in turn, pulled me aside one night to tell me how much he liked Tony, that his wife had told him what a "handsome man" he was (!) and he found him to be a very intelligent, caring and empathic person. He was very happy for me. On our last night there before leaving for Winnipeg, Tony had planned out (with me as his sous chef) a grand dinner he prepared for the family. It was a fitting end to our visit. We left the next morning, eager to see my Dad.

I knew it was going to be hard on Tony meeting my father for the first time, as he wanted so much to make a good impression. The kids were excited to see their grandfather and we arrived at the hotel to our 2 separate but adjoining rooms. We weren't sure how the kids would take to us being in a room together, but they were excited at the freedom to be on their own next door. We dressed quickly for dinner to meet my Dad and his wife at a restaurant close by. Tony looked so handsome in a suit with shirt-and-tie and my Dad greeted him warmly. The kids were thrilled to see their grandfather and chatted excitedly with him and his wife. She is a very "proper" lady with a tinkly laugh and ladylike mannerisms with whom my father had blossomed back into life again after losing my mother. Tony easily charmed both of them, and my father called me at the hotel later that night to say how impressed he was with him, what a special man he was. It was such a relief for him to see how happy I was again, loved by a caring man.

There was another reason to be going to Winnipeg at that time. Our trip coincided with my 25th high school reunion. I had no intention of going, being the "poor-kid-on-the-block" who was ostracized by the few girls in my class. My parents had me apply to the school and write the entrance exam because I was so bored in public school. Although it had been a private boys' school for over a century, they had decided to make it co-ed a few years before. With a class of 50 boys and 10 girls, I was accepted and got the best score on the entrance exam, winning a scholarship. Without that, there was no way my parents could have afforded to send me. I thrived on the academic stimulation in the school that was like a British boarding school. The "masters", as they were called were hand-picked by the head-master and were brilliant educators. They challenged our young minds, which was exciting and invigorating, but at the same time the school was dedicated to academic excellence, it was also encouraging sporting prowess. I adored it all: rugby, football, soccer, Australian football, field hockey, cross-country, ice hockey, volleyball, basketball, tennis and even more. I loved the sports and earned the nickname "Killer" for my aggressiveness on the basketball court and inability to stop in ice hockey until I smashed into someone. I guess I would have been classified a "book-worm jock", as although I wasn't great at many of the sports, I'd play anything. The best part of the sports was that they were co-ed and the guys didn't seem to hold back.

The school social life had been another matter...I had no problem with any of the guys and they easily accepted me, but not most of the girls. Many were from wealthy families and wearing designer clothes (which I had never seen in my life) was a daily wardrobe for them, but I had made many of my own clothes to take the burden off my family financially and the girls regarded me in disdain. I was a bit of an odd-ball socially and I guess I had carried that monkey-on-my-back for years.

When I had told Tony about the reunion, which I had no intention of attending, he said it was time I went, with my head-held-high. I had made a good life for myself, had a great education, career and business, and there was nothing to be uncomfortable about. I was worried that the stigma of divorce, feeling like a failure, would haunt me but he reminded me that I had a new lease on life, not to view myself as a relationship loser. So, I had packed some of my new "designer" clothes, ready to brave the storm.

There were a number of get-togethers, the first of which was a barbecue at the head-master's house. The kids, Tony and I arrived there and they were amazed at the opulence of the school grounds, multiple buildings and property. On arrival at the barbecue, immediately my old sports buddies recognized me and were thrilled to see me. While I chatted with the guys, Tony made himself busy making balloon creatures for the little kids who were there. As he was considerably younger that the rest of us, the parents assumed that he had been hired as entertainment for the kids and he found this hilarious.

The women were another matter. Many stared at me haughtily, clearly gossiping about me being divorced (I suspected). Sharing a few beers with the guys (Tony was driving), we shared tales of our sporting endeavours (I was renowned for having "canned" the ex-head-master in a soccer game by mistake in a masters/students game). It all felt so comfortable and easy until, sliding easily into another group, we all recognized each other, save for one woman. I introduced myself to her and asked whose wife she was. "Oh, I recognize you, you haven't changed at all", she smirked. It was one of the girls from my class, who I wouldn't have recognized at all. Awkward…the guys laughed it off and Tony watched appreciatively.

We were invited to a barbecue at one of their homes the next night, sans kids (the kids happily stayed at my Dad's). As I dressed carefully for the evening, Tony commented on how he had seen everyone respond to me with genuine interest and affection, except for the women…"they're just jealous", he said, "because you're still hot and they look like middle-aged moms". Bolstered by his compliment, we arrived looking quite the stylish couple. Everyone was, again, so pleasant and engaging. I even got hit on by several of my ex-class-mates and one of the wives asked me what her husband had been like as a teen. He and I had dated for a while and she appeared to be almost anxious about it. I reassured her that I was still just a kid when I was in high-school and dating to me had been simply about outings to the park or bike-rides or going to plays or concerts or debating world issues with our friends…nothing ever serious, which was true. She seemed relieved and the evening was a big success.

It seemed that many had taken a long time to "find themselves" and with the cushion of their parents' fortunes, they had the luxury of taking that time. They seemed to be quite impressed with how I had taken my education and run with it, creating a career and thriving business out of it but not surprised, as they had seen my inner turmoil and drive to succeed. It was a wonderful revelation, being able to see myself through others' eyes at that time and I am eternally grateful to Tony for encouraging me to confront my fears of ghosts from the past.

Our visit with Dad and his wife had been a great time to catch up for the kids, Dad and me, and Tony was so warmly received. Friends of Dad's from England had been visiting and we had a lovely meal with them at a restaurant where he took pictures of us all at the table. Looking back now at that moment-in-time captured in the photos, it was a very happy and close time for us all. When we got back home, Dad gave me a call a few nights later to tell me (he wasn't supposed to, but he was too excited), that while we had been there, Tony had asked Dad for my hand in marriage and he had been thrilled to give his consent. "Well-raised, that young man!" Dad had enthused, making me promise not to tell.

Back at home, I told the kids that Tony and I were looking to buy a home together for us all (at least, 50% of the time for them). They weren't thrilled to possibly move out of the neighbourhood as many of their friends lived nearby, but I promised them it would still be close, and I'd drive them to friends or pick up friends if the weather was bad. So, Tony and I started looking in earnest.

In the middle of all this one night when the kids were with me and Tony was over at my town-house, David had had a few friends over and they were listening to music in his basement rooms. I went down just to check on them and found David belligerent and obnoxious. Asking him to come out of the room and talk so as not to embarrass him, I noticed everyone had gone quiet. Glancing back, I saw a partially empty mickey of alcohol thrown under his bed and told him it was time for his friends to leave. He angrily refused, and I asked them, myself.

After they had sullenly left, I told David that he was grounded while I thought about things. I realized that in feeling bad for the kids, I had let up a bit too much in the discipline. While Tony sat inconspicuously listening in the living-room, David had a melt-down and insisted on calling his father. I relented, and he screeched to his father about how "mean" I was being. "He says to come over, I'm not grounded there!" David smirked triumphantly. I asked him to speak to his father and told him that there needed to be some guidelines, some changes. Jeff smugly responded that if I kept a "hard line", I'd lose the kids eventually. I stood there with my jaw hanging open as David flounced out the door to be picked up by his father. It was weeks before he would even respond to my phone calls and I was devastated. In the meantime, Jackie continued to stay on their weeks with me and kept me up on how David was doing.

But Jackie was having her issues, too. Her favourite elementary school teacher, who had put her in the gifted education program, had recommended her for the same in junior high. She was outright refusing, saying that she didn't want to be "different" anymore, was tired of being seen as a "geek". I decided to lay off for the summer break and to revisit the issue when school was to begin again at the end of the summer. Little did I know that again, behind my back, Jeff was creating a quagmire for me. He had told her that in no uncertain terms, if she wanted to be in the regular program, he would support her. It would be a tougher year than I even realized, but in the meantime, Tony and I had found a lovely split-level house just a few blocks out of the old neighbourhood that had a great back yard and more than enough room for the 4 of us. We put in an offer and it was accepted, for us to move in a week before his 30th birthday.

Reconnecting with the business community had been interesting, with a new business name and contact numbers. I had decided to change my name back to my maiden name, wanting to disassociate myself from Jeff and his antics. Some of them did find me, and I had a consultation with a previous client at his offices one day. Always a shrewd customer, he looked over his glasses at me and asked about how things were going with Jeff and the "other, other woman". Surprised, I asked him what he meant. "Everyone in the business knows about the latest and commiserates with you. Few people really liked or respected Jeff after we found out about Barb in the first place," he continued. Confused, I asked: "What about Barb? She's his lawyer I know, and we were all friends once, which I know isn't quite kosher for her to be his lawyer now". "You mean you don't know? No one ever told you that Jeff had an affair with Barb? Everyone knew about it," he replied, looking astonished. I stared at him with my jaw hanging open and then some of the pieces fell into place...Jeff and Barb had gone to a conference together for a weekend, ostensibly to make some business connections in the U.S. together. As I thought back, it began to make sense, as Jeff had returned with a "present" for me from Rodeo Drive, a sequined jacket he said Barb had been jealous of. He had her try it on to check on the size and because she's short and dumpy, it looked awful on her, but he had thought it would look "great" on me. He'd never, ever bought me a surprise present before and I had treasured it as perhaps a peace-offering, a new beginning...guess it was, but in the wrong way. Soon after that, Jeff had completely turned off, rarely talking to me and his later-night "work" had begun.

More pieces of the past puzzle were fitting into place and I felt even more naïve and stupid. Stupid, stupid me...trying so hard to fix things: his relationship with the kids, his relationship with his family before that, our relationship. In the meantime, he had already been "doing his own thing" for a long time. He had had no intention of "fixing things" with me, and instead had gone on and made himself a new life apart from the kids and me. All of that wasted time, energy and anguish I had put into trying to make a better, happier life for our little family. He had certainly been right when he had told me so many years before that there was a side of him I would never know…

I had planned a surprise party for Tony with his brothers, who made sure to invite the whole family. I had met his parents once, at a little Easter party they were having at their house. His mother had suggested that he may as well invite me, so that she could get to know me, but she didn't want to meet the kids yet. That was and still is a sore point for her, that I had kids and was divorced. She didn't even care for poor old Jack at first, as she saw him as a tie to my ex- (!), although Jeff had shown little interest in seeing him since we had split. The few times he had come to the door to pick up the kids at transition time, Jack had joyously greeted him at the door (he always stayed outside), but Jeff had never done so much as pat him or even acknowledge him. It was a confusing and sad time for my poor old pup, as his tail would go down, his eyes would dull, and he'd skulk away to lie on my bed. It took some time, but eventually Jack didn't even respond when the door-bell rang with Jeff there to pick up the kids. When David had exiled himself at his father's, Jack had a difficult time with the arrival of Jackie for their week-on, sniffing around pathetically looking for David at the same time. He would look anxious when there were arguments, his tail anxiously wagging as it drooped, trying to nudge whoever was angry into submission with a gentle poke of his nose.

The party at Tony's parents had been uncomfortable. In a panic about what to wear, what to say, what not to say, Tony had gently held my face in his hands and told me that: "They're going to love you, everyone does. Look at my younger brothers, you're already like a big sister to them, sometimes they want to see you more than me!!!". So we arrived, bearing a gift of a cake I had made. His father quietly accepted it and his mother stared at me coolly. It turned out that Tony's father was a plant enthusiast and their house was filled with all types of plants, to his mother's exasperation. He took me on a tour and excitedly told me about each one. We chatted comfortably for a long time while his family looked on. Tony's older sister was visiting from Saskatchewan with her family and the kids and I took to each other quickly. The same went for his sister and her family who lived here in Vancouver. Both women were most open, warm and welcoming to me, as we had motherhood in common and their naturally gentle natures shone through.

They all seemed surprised at how long and animated my conversation had been with their Dad. Tony's mother had quietly noted this and kept herself busy getting the family fed. She asked me a few pointed questions about my kids, my business and the divorce, giving little feedback but seemingly storing the information for later. After I made sure to do the dishes and thanked his parents for their kindness at inviting me, Tony and I left. He was amazed, he later told me, at how much his father had spoken to me, as he rarely spoke to anyone much. He had a strong accent and apparently some people had problems understanding him, but I had grown up in a family with grandparents and elderly aunts and uncles whose accents from the old country had never left them. It was natural for me.

We moved into our new house at the beginning of the summer. My town-house was still up for sale, as was the marital house that Jeff still lived in with the kids being there half of the time. It was very upsetting for me to have to keep up with 3 mortgages now, waiting for the others to sell. I think that Jeff quite enjoyed still being there, knowing that it was squeezing me financially. Our real estate agent (as we later discovered) had been touting the house as "a good deal, they're in a messy divorce and just want to get rid of it," much to my chagrin.

Jeff had called me to meet about some "financial matters" before the move, which I had agreed to, hoping for some resolution to our dead-lock on the divorce. When I arrived at the coffee-shop, he had some papers he wanted me to sign. Again, he was asking me to co-sign a bridge-loan for him to buy a place, as he sneered "I don't have my parents around to loan me money for a down-payment". Flabbergasted, I refused. Why should I do him any favours? He was the one who had started things in motion by his unwillingness to work on the marriage…he left in a huff. As I mentioned, I had discovered later, when I looked at the limited disclosure he had given to my lawyer, that the amount he had been asking me to co-sign for was for 2 houses…one for him and one he was buying to rent out to Julia!!! I didn't realize this at the time, but if I had known, I would have really lost it!!! The nerve of him…it still makes my blood pressure rise when I think of him having the gall to try to get me to help him get the house for her, as well!!! Just goes to show the unscrupulous nature of the man…

Chapter 12: Tony

How can I begin to describe Tony? When I first met him, he surprised me by his candour. Like myself, he explained later, he had nothing to hide. He loved his family, especially his two younger brothers, who he had taken under his wing due to the age-difference between them and the older siblings. Tony adored his many nephews and one niece and spent considerable time finding them "just the right presents" for their birthdays and Christmas. When there were family get-togethers, he couldn't wait to joke with them and play games.

With his father, Tony had a quietly loving relationship. His dad was proud of his education, career and accomplishments and Tony greatly respected his father's personal sacrifices to bring them to this country. His dad had played quite a big role in helping to raise the kids, which was quite unusual for their generation and Tony still laughed at remembering his father desperately trying to get all 6 kids fed at breakfast before school. Tony's relationship with his mother was a much more complicated one. She ran the household and had been the disciplinarian. Tony had been one of her major targets. Being a kid caught between 2 cultures, his natural independence and need for autonomy were at odds with her need for absolute control. While his older siblings had "towed the line" with old-country values, Tony had embraced his new country. He hadn't been a disrespectful or wilful child, but he was outspoken and independent, wanting to fit into his new country with new friends.

Money had been tight for the family when he was first here in Canada and there hadn't been much to help support his love of sports, but Tony had taken odd-jobs and saved throughout his childhood to pay for any extra-curricular activities with school and/or sports that his parents couldn't afford.

As a shy, quiet child outside of the home, Tony's self-esteem and confidence had come through sports. He was also a quick-study, easily learning English and school subjects. When it came to homework, however, he never wanted to do it because he felt he had already learned what he needed to from assignments in school and this caused much frustration for his teachers and then punishment from his mother. The arrival of his two younger brothers had changed the family dynamics considerably, the first born here in Canada. The family was doing much better financially, so Tim and Todd grew up with less discipline and more resources. Tony had watched the world his little brothers grow up in with some dismay compared to how he had been raised, but he never begrudged them and was always supportive and loving towards them. Their love and admiration of him was always so clear.

Tony's religion, being a Roman Catholic, was very important to him. The values, morals and ethics he had learned through his religious upbringing were very much a part of him, but he still managed to maintain his scientific principles and integrate them together. He had thought a lot about it and thought a lot about just about everything. I had never met a person who seemed more prepared for every situation and he explained that was because he always worked through every possible scenario for any given (and hypothetical) situation in advance.

Tony was extremely athletic and had been offered numerous basketball scholarships, one of them to UCLA but he had refused it at the time (much to his regret now) because he thought he would be home-sick for his family. How sweet was that: a sentimental academic who's not ashamed of it. He had played for the local university team with some success and now helped coach his younger brothers on their high school teams.

Being a shy kid in school, Tony had some friends, but most were through sports. He really came into his own to become the self-confident person he is today because of the jobs and friends he had when he had graduated from high school. His first job after that was supposed to be as a cook or dishwasher in a Mexican chain restaurant, but instead they put him on his first shift after extensive training as a server. When he arrived for that shift and discovered he was to wait on tables, he had begged to work in the back kitchen, but they told him it was serve or wait until a kitchen job came up. Tony's description of that first shift, as he got a nose-bleed from the stress of waiting on his first table and ended up locking himself in the bathroom out of embarrassment, then being talked into returning to the table is so far beyond unrecognizable from the man I had met and come to love.

As hospitality staff frequently do, he was invited along to a bar with the guys after a shift. When he was left alone that first time, Tony described not knowing what to do with himself, as he had never been alone in a crowd, having to meet people on his own. The guys had ordered shots when they first arrived and Tony, never having done it before, started sipping his (it tasted awful to him) while they pounded theirs back. They explained to him that the object was to "shoot it back". So he did and then they had gone off to their own devices. It had definitely been a defining moment for him, and he resolved to himself that he didn't want to be shy anymore, so pushed himself to introduce himself to people after that. The friendships that he formed with co-workers have remained and grown stronger, many of them even closer to him than some of his family. Even their families consider him a second- or third-son and he is invited to all of their family gatherings.

Friendships were one thing, but relationships with women were another. Tony's shyness got in the way of him dating much in high school. After becoming more outgoing and eventually working as a bartender in numerous establishments while going to university, he became quite the ladies' man. Although he admits to dating a lot of women, most of them were not well-received by his friends. And his mother hadn't appreciated any of them. One in particular he had gone out with for 3 years and he had tried to break up with her, but she had attempted to kill herself by overdosing on pills, so he decided to move in with her and stayed with her for another 3 years until he felt she was strong enough for them to break up. That was the kind of man he was: loyal, caring and compassionate. But after that break-up, he admitted to going through a bit of a "bastard phase" with women, as some he had cared for before and after her had dumped him unceremoniously without warning and he didn't know who to trust. Then he had met me…

Growing up with hand-me-downs from his older brother and older cousins, Tony had longed for some things of his own and resolved to have a different life. While he was working many hours at various jobs and graduated with his second degree before going onto his doctorate, he had moved into a down-town loft apartment. He still reminisced about the chic, ultra-modern urban feel of it with the new modernistic furniture he bought to treat himself. He managed to stay there for less than a year before he had to come back to earth and go into student residences in order to be able to afford the final phase of his education. But he still had some of that furniture, very sparse, modern and masculine, in his duplex when we met.

His dressing style was immaculate and designer…clean, European lines and not fussy. I had never met a man who spent more time on his hair and nails. Tony maintained a hair-style he had figured out for himself near the end of high school. It suited him immensely, how he coiffed and gelled it, but he never trusted his hair to a stylist or barber. To my surprise, his mother still cut his hair and this task was to fall to me after some time together, although I don't think his mother ever forgave me for taking it away from her.

I had never seen Tony angry but was surprised one morning to hear him screaming on his phone downstairs at my townhouse. Luckily the kids weren't there, and I quickly retreated back upstairs until he was finished. I had heard screaming on the other end of the line and knew it had been a woman. Turns out it was his mother and hence the complicated relationship I have alluded to. She was still trying to control him, complaining and criticizing and he apologized profusely when I finally came downstairs. "She just knows how to provoke me…it's infuriating!" Tony was still on edge. When I got to know her later (and we did get along later), she confided in me that she had many regrets about how she had treated Tony growing up, that she hadn't been close or nurturing enough and had been so tough on him.

Tony was a very successful businessman, having left a position at a hospital early on in his career and setting up his own practice. He had brought in other associates who worked their own practices at his offices and from whom he received part of their earnings. It was amazing to hear how he had begun out of one office on his own and quickly built up a reputation for himself as a smart, honest, hard worker with great integrity and others had come to join in his success. He was, like me, the first entrepreneur in his family and this scared his parents because they had always worked for someone (albeit very hard, where he clearly learned his work-ethic) until their retirement, with the security of a pension. They didn't quite "get" the whole psychology thing and didn't see it as a viable occupation.

The Tony I met was very different from who he was growing up. He had grown himself from humble, shy beginnings into a successful, charismatic, independent, popular and outgoing man. His compassion and caring he had learned from his love and caring for and from his family and extended family friends and his own life and relationship experiences. He learned from everything, he explained to me, never to make the same mistake twice. Opening up his simple life and huge heart to me was a big gamble, but he knew, he told me, from almost our first night together that I was "the one". And we haven't looked back since...

Chapter 13: A New Kind of Family...

The kids were excited about the move and staked out their rooms. We promised both that we would paint them to their taste. We had a "house-warming party" that I had secretly planned as Tony's 30th and it was great fun. In a house filled with some of the kids' friends, Tony's and my friends, his family and some neighbours we had invited. The hot summer day was perfect. Some people had brought their swim-suits to go in the hot-tub, and the beer flowed freely. Tony's parents arrived early, his Dad marvelling at my plants and his mother proceeded to search through my kitchen cupboards. She was surprised, she noted, to find my collection of Italian dishes and table-ware, as well as how many Italian specialty spices and foods I had in my fridge and pantry. I explained to her that it was just about my favourite food and she seemed impressed, if quieted. As Jackie trotted by (I had introduced the kids to her as soon as they had arrived), Tony's mother had patted Jackie on the bottom, commenting that it looked like she liked to eat Italian food. The expression of surprise and stupefaction on Jackie's face was priceless and I later explained to her that it was Tony's mother's way of showing her interest in her (I thought?).

All seemed to be going okay in our new home. With the divorce still no further ahead and me miserable every day I went to work, Tony suggested I move my office to our home. He would build an office space for me in our attached garage so that I could work out-of-home on my own schedule, away from the tension of Jeff. Alixe had finally quit working for us and Jeff and I were doing all of our own clerical, calls, and appointments now. He was jealously not giving me my messages, although I continued to dutifully give him his. It was almost open war-fare at the business, and clients would anxiously ask me not to ever refer me to Jeff or have him do any work for them. In turn, his clients would walk down the hallway to his office, giving me vicious stares as I later learned he was spending part of his business time telling them about how mean and terrible I was to him(?!)...and he was spreading rumours in the business community about my credibility and mental health, which I discovered a few years later.

Tony set about finishing the garage space as an office and waiting-room. The neighbours (I thought inquisitive but friendly) took quite an interest in what we were doing. Several even leant us some tools and one volunteered to drill through the garage wall into the basement to connect the heat to the garage from the house. It took a month and its toll on Tony's sleep (I found him fast asleep on the carpet in the garage one morning after pulling an all-nighter), but finally it was done. The kids had even helped, breaking up the drywall on the walls to be replaced. I had already changed my name back to my maiden-name, wanting to avoid the controversy that was swirling in the business community about Jeff's honesty and business activities. I had heard through the grape-vine that he was regarded as quite a shark, swooping in on businesses that already had their own advertising contracts, to low-ball them and get them to switch.

I had already told Jeff that I wanted to leave the business building with him and asked for an equitable solution of splitting the phone/fax lines, but he had stubbornly refused. In frustration, seeing how hopeless I felt about the situation, Tony suggested that why shouldn't I just move out and leave him there on his own to pay the lease, if he wasn't going to be fair? It made sense to me, although I was nervous at the prospect of meeting Jeff as I packed things up. Tony and several of his friends showed up one night to help me move out my half of the files, of the office supplies, my desk and filing cabinet. Just for good measure, as we left, Tony said we were taking the coffee-maker and small bar-fridge, as we had left Jeff all the office furniture and computers, the board-room table and most of the waiting-room furniture. It was with shaky hands that I locked up for the last time, pushing my set of keys under the door to the office suite. I had taken a few days off to transition and called my clients about the change in address, for them to meet at my new office-space. Calling the phone company, they were not willing to help in any way with the phone or fax lines, as they were under Jeff's name, so I had to start all over again.

It was about to get even dirtier…Jeff called me screaming the next day, threatening me with having to pay for half of the new lease. I tried to stay calm as I told him that he kept the business and offices under his name (no longer mine), as well as the phones and fax lines, so I wasn't taking any responsibility for them anymore. He ranted and raved, threatened to make things even worse with the divorce (as if it wasn't already bad enough), and I was shaking by the time I got off the phone. Even the kids were accusatory when they arrived for their week with me, as clearly Jeff had done a number on me to them about how mean and unreasonable I was being.

Jackie had begun her new junior high school and I got a call from the school asking me to meet with the principal. Apparently, she was refusing to join the gifted classroom, saying she wanted to be in a "normal" class. I begged the principal to give it a chance for a few days. In the meantime, Jeff had met with the school and said that he "only wanted what was best" for Jackie, that if she wasn't happy to be in the gifted program, he supported her decision. She was at Jeff's that first week and had refused to get up to go to school or answer my calls but left me emails that I was being "mean" and "not listening" to her. Finally, after a week when the school called me every day and I was painted as the pushy, mean parent, I relented and she began school, in the "normal" (as she called it) program. It was a bad mistake on my part in retrospect, but it seemed that I was having to fight everyone for everything…to regain my credibility in the business world, to fight with the kids over the lack of discipline and unlimited money that their father carelessly threw at them, to keep spending money on lawyers who were stone-walled by Jeff's legal shark, to try and get the other houses sold and no longer draining me so much financially…it seemed never-ending.

In the midst of this, my Dad called me one night. He was becoming even more frustrated than me at the state of my divorce and had asked to read through the papers my lawyer was working on. He had noticed that Jeff was listed as "divorced", what did that mean? I was forced to tell him that I had lied that many years ago when they had met Jeff, not telling the full story that he had already been married and divorced once. Dad was disappointed, but I tried to explain that I felt (rightly) that they didn't like him from the beginning and he didn't need more strikes against him at that time. I quickly reassured Dad that I should have listened, he and my mother had been right…but Dad countered with then he wouldn't have his wonderful grandchildren, and all seemed right again. He did say that he wanted to come to Vancouver and interview other lawyers with me, promising to help me with the financial part of getting the divorce finished. He knew it was slowly draining me emotionally, financially and health-wise.

Dad and Tony had a wonderful time staying up late nights talking when he arrived, and Tony quickly told me that he had never met a person more caring, supportive and honest with him who wasn't in his family. Together, we went to meet several high-profile lawyers in town and Dad grilled them on what they'd do differently. The one we chose was going to get a forensic accountant to try and find what had happened to our money, which we suspected Jeff had funnelled through the trust account he had left open from his mother in his name. We needed proof that cheques were going into it in order to have the account opened for inspection…and I did find several cheques from our banking records that had gone into the account, but the accountant maintained that it was not enough "proof" to request having the account opened for inspection. Jeff had won again…

Dad had left the initial down-payment with my new lawyer, who in the end proved to be too busy to do much on my case. He rarely returned my phone-calls, kept charging for unanswered letters, calls and emails to Jeff's lawyer and in the end, I relented and returned to the lawyer in my former building. It was frustrating beyond belief, but there was nothing I could do. Asking for disclosure of properties, I saw that Jeff had bought both his and Julia's properties (asking the kids Julia's address, it was the same as the other property he owned), I put the cost of the two properties together and then I understood the amount Jeff had asked me to co-sign the bridge loan for…both his new place and the one he was renting to Julia. On the phone that night with Dad, I wept bitterly at my stupidity at marrying Jeff in the first place, but he reminded me that "there was a place in hell for people like that".

It turned out that the neighbours weren't so "friendly" after all. I received a notice in the mail from the city that they had called Bylaw Enforcement on me for having a business on the property. They wanted to "examine my records", but when I called them back I refused to give them personal details of my clients and explained that my business didn't bring much traffic to the area, only a few cars a day. It turned out that an old lady several doors up was keeping records of the car license plates of any car that came to our house…even the pizza or Chinese take-out vehicles!!! I approached each of the neighbours to explain the issue and try to resolve the issue, but they would not relent. A "public hearing" was to be held but I was to be away visiting my Aunt and Uncle in Winnipeg and Tony promised he'd attend to represent me, the dear, as if he hadn't already done enough!

It turns out the concerns were "increased traffic", and I was admonished to reduce the visitation, but Tony suggested that if we built a double garage with access to the back-lane, it wouldn't impact on anyone and they relented. But it didn't stop there, as even when we had built it, the old lady kept driving up and down the lane throughout the day, recording license plates. It came to a point where I asked the local police to try to mediate the problem and although the officer offered to have a mediation meeting with them, the neighbours refused. I ended up telling him I'd charge them with criminal harassment if the "monitoring" continued and it became a very unfriendly detente living in that neighbourhood.

With the divorce still driving me nuts, the miserable neighbour situation, and trying to regain my business again, the least I needed was more troubles but sure enough, they came. One night, arguing again with Jackie about getting her homework done (she wasn't bringing home any, but I had found the school website that her teachers posted it on), she was beyond being rude and disrespectful. Tony had resolved to let me "handle things" with the kids, being the "boyfriend" and not the parent, but he just couldn't take how Jackie was treating me. He calmly walked into the room and suggested that we take a breather (for which I was thankful). Jackie sullenly skulked away and he followed her, trying to talk to her about being responsible, not disrespecting her mother. She got quietly mouthy and Tony told her she should write some "lines" about how she should "not disrespect her mother".

It was a great idea and I had never imposed any discipline like that, but after writing it a few times, she refused to do anymore. When I insisted that it was a good idea, she started screaming and called her father about how terribly she was being treated. And guess what? Jeff said he was coming over to get her…seeing how angry I was, Tony tried to negotiate with Jeff over the phone but to no avail and so Jackie flounced out of the house, not to return for another 8 months.

David kept coming throughout that time but refused to tell me how Jackie was doing. I tried keeping up with Jackie by phone, email, through the school (checking with teachers as to how she was doing…horribly). She was sleeping in over at Jeff's or "going to school" and returning home to sleep after he left for work and her attendance was abominable. I tried to reason with him via email (as phone calls just ended up in screaming matches), but Jeff wouldn't do anything about it.

In the meantime, David had begun high school and a new job at the pizza place near our house. We weren't thrilled with him working yet, but he wanted the pocket money. It was hard to refuse, but he did listen when we asked him to limit his work hours on week-nights. I would drive him home from work when he was tired or there and back when it was cold out. Keeping up with parent-teachers at the high school was tough, as David didn't want to attend the meetings and Jeff never showed any interest in going, so I dutifully went and kept notes to email to him so that he could encourage David from his end.

The school had a very dedicated Assistant Principal who took up the cause with David and she and I worked hard together to keep up his interest and work with the teachers. Just like Jackie, he had refused to enter into the gifted program and he was slacking, but some of his teachers were willing to "get creative" with him to make assignments more interesting. I tried to keep up with his friends, having them over during his weeks with me, but I could feel David slipping…he wouldn't join any after-school or extra-curricular activities and preferred to "hang out" with his friends, none of whom showed any interest in school or anything else. Between Jackie refusing to stay over anymore, sending me angry emails and David withdrawing even further, I felt I was losing my children and myself as a mother.

Motherhood, wife and business-woman had been my order-of-priorities in life. My own mother had stopped working when she had me, even though I had often encouraged her to return to work when Garry and I were older. I saw her aimlessness, her lack of direction and loneliness that had contributed to her alcoholism and when I'd left home for grad school, I had bought her driving lessons to get her out-and-about. She never went, cashing them in to buy alcohol after I left. My father had been a saint to weather the storm of life with her, as it was rarely a happy place. Although she encouraged my academic endeavours, there were always accusations, verbal punishment and abuse from her when I would come home after working long hours at university and my jobs. I would fall into bed exhausted for a couple of hours sleep and she'd wander into my room, turn on the lights most nights and berate me that she "knew more in her pinkie finger" about business than I'd ever know.

Needless to say, living with that negativity was tough and moving away for grad school was a breath-of-fresh-air, but I never felt I could leave until Garry was strong and old enough to endure it. Sometimes I think that I connected so fast with Jeff away from home because I needed to be a part of something, to cope with the guilt and emotional abuse heaped on me from afar by my mom over the phone in our weekly calls. Rarely was she sober or positive, and I used to dread those calls...

I had resolved to be as positive a parent as there could be with my kids, but in retrospect, I had made them my life. Any activity they wanted to do, I'd find it and join in whole-heartedly as a parent or coach or assistant or volunteer of any sort. Guess I was compensating for the isolation I felt as a kid with my mother not driving or being able to enrol me in much. Any pet they wanted (within reason), I could justify as a learning experience for them and I would end up looking after (I never learned). That included several budgies (both David and Jackie had one, but Jack had unfortunately attacked one of Jackie's and I'd had to get another), a lizard (Xera), a corn snake (but she needed a friend, so we got her a male rat-snake), albino African pygmy hedge-hogs (they kept having babies), 3 tiny African tree-frogs (Hewey, Dewey and Louie, not my fault as they were a gift from a friend for David's birthday...who gives kids pets for gifts?!), and several mice (given to me to feed the snakes by a friend's daughter, but the kids couldn't bear to feed them to the snakes).

Again, maybe I was compensating for not being able to have pets growing up (my mother said any creature other than human was a "filthy creature" and I used to long for any pet). When Jeff and I had split, I couldn't fit all the pets into my town-house and so the snakes went to a friend's friend who was a herpetologist, the birds had (thankfully) passed on to higher places, the same went for the mice and the hedge-hogs went to a friend of Jackie's. I kept the lizard and Jeff said he'd take care of the 3 little frogs, but I learned from the kids that he wouldn't ever go out to get them the crickets they needed to survive, so the poor little things died.

The kids didn't care about their pets anymore and would rarely walk Jack. When I had suggested that they help with cleaning up the back-yard after him, they refused, as "Dad has pooper-people come, why should we have to here?" The same went for Jackie's lizard, a gentle little creature that I would play with to keep her amused. Tony had been a little overwhelmed with the menagerie when we had met but had accepted it as one of my many eccentricities. With Jackie refusing to come over anymore, I left her a message that I was going to drop off her lizard at her father's, for him to take care of. After doing so, she triumphantly left me a message that he had "adopted her out" to a nearby pet store. I couldn't win. No matter how I had tried to encourage the kids to take responsibility for things in their lives, for the creatures they took on, to their coaches and teachers, they simply refused.

I had failed as a mother, all of my hopes and dreams for the kids, what I had tried to achieve with them and for them felt like it had all drained away. I had already been slapped in the face with having failed as a wife. Tony saw my desolation and as much as I loved our relationship, he knew that I was losing a big piece of me. He suggested we open a business together, perhaps to fill the void. A night-club/bar had come on sale in the downtown area. What did I know about the bar business? Very little, other than one of my jobs in university having been a waitress at a bar. Tony had worked his way through university by working at bars around the city and had even helped a colleague open his own bar. So, we resolved to figure out how to make it happen. He sold his duplex and my town-house had sold, so we combined the money to buy it. We were so excited!!!

It had been an alternative bar with a very specialized reputation and we wanted to make it more chic, more main-stream. Putting our heads together, we decided on the renovations we were going to make and tried to hire as many of their staff as wanted to continue, to maintain their clientele, with the owner's blessings. They had had enough of the business and just wanted to retire to warmer climates. In retrospect, we should have been much more wary of the building leasing manager, as he sat us down, offering us a Scotch at the lease-signing…little did we know that he was an angry drunk, who would rotate around the building owner's properties throughout the day getting drunker and more belligerent as he went.

Tony had taken a couple of weeks off of his business to do the renovations and I had done the same. We managed to meet our deadline of re-opening within 11 days of switching ownership, much to the credit of Tony, who hardly slept the whole time and stayed over at the building most nights to work round-the-clock.

We had (we thought) really thought through what the city was missing...an up-scale, chic and different venue. We had a custom aquarium built for near the entrance, complete with exotic rays and other tropical fish, go-go-dancers, a private area for bottle-service (never before done in the city, it was Tony's idea from his travels to L.A.), 2 levels of music and 4 bars spread throughout the 2 floors. Little did we know that there would be troubles from within, as well as outside problems from the drunken building manager...

Chapter 14: Life Gets More Confusing (if possible!)

We began with a good business following. I had found some good outlets for advertising (both free, as I got us in the "New Business" section of the newspaper on its front page, but quite costly on the radio). We became known as an ethnically-mixed, open venue where people just had to show respect for the place and our staff to be welcome. There were some challenges within from early on, however, as we soon realized our door-staff were "greasing" at the door, contrary to our specific directions.

Given that it was quite a large place, we really needed our bouncers to keep things calm and safe, but they did everything they could to try and make money on the side. Firing the first, then the second head door-man, it became clear that the crew was trying to undermine our authority and our clientele. Several vicious fights that they could have stopped or prevented began to give us a reputation as a dangerous place, far from what we had envisioned. Tony and I struggled to keep afloat while we closed for several weeks to revamp the place again and try to start fresh, but after the first year, it was beyond exhausting.

One night while I was downstairs in the office at the club going through receipts, I got a call from Dad that he needed to talk to me privately. He tearfully explained to me that the cancer he had managed to beat the years ago with having his kidney removed had returned. The doctors had caught it in the routine scan they had done in preparation for his hip surgery, but they hadn't told him about it until after the surgery was done and he had recovered. I was devastated but tried not to show him my panic, struggling to remain calm on the phone.

Unfortunately, there were few treatment alternatives available. Dad had been diagnosed with Myasthenia Gravis soon after I had left Jeff. He had been losing weight and the doctors couldn't seem to figure it out. His wife had had to call the ambulance as he would choke on his medications. Although I had just been getting my business going again, I knew I had to go and help. When I arrived, I had found Dad a shadow of his former self. He had little mobility or energy to dress himself and his wife showed little interest. I took it upon myself to set up meetings with his doctors and push them for a diagnosis…was it Lou Gehrig's disease or Parkinson's? They finally diagnosed it as Myasthenia Gravis, when a person's white blood cells attack a healthy part of the body's muscles. Dad's was his tongue, so he had problems talking, drinking and eating.

It was heart-breaking to see the big strong father I knew as the walking skeleton he had become. I pressured the docs for a solution. They decided to try a really high dose of Prednisone to trigger a quick response (little did I know that they had given my Dad less than a few weeks to live at that point). Miraculously it worked, and Dad's symptoms abated completely but I knew there was trouble coming with his wife…

While staying over at Dad's with her since Dad had to be in hospital for a few days, his usually upbeat (if not impersonal and often sweetly sarcastic) wife informed me that she was "sick of taking care of a sick man"! She had taken care of her previous husband, who had been much older than her when she married him, until he died. When she and my father had decided to marry, she made him "promise" that he was healthy and wouldn't get sick?! Well, he was healthy when they married, but this new illness was not planned and I stared at her open-mouthed, seething inside at this woman's selfishness. She hadn't minded my father footing the bill for building her a house big enough for her home-business, nor had she minded him taking her on trips she had never been on in her life, nor had she minded him taking her out to fancy restaurants and buying her designer clothes and jewellery…what had Dad gotten himself into?

So, having had one relapse of the symptoms of Myasthenia Gravis, Dad was not able to have any surgery to remove the cancer they had found in his lung. This auto-immune disorder also meant that he could not take radiation treatment or traditional chemotherapy. He had found out about a research trial that was ongoing in Winnipeg with a new medication regimen and had signed himself up for it. He seemed to be feeling hopeful that it would work.

Tony was devastated to hear of Dad's condition and gave me every support possible, saying that if I ever needed to go to Dad or have him there, he would do anything to help. The calls to the kids were tough ones, as they had lost the other 3 grandparents in their lives.

As David was only coming over sporadically now, I couldn't wait until he might show up. Jackie was still refusing to visit.

It had been a tough year, but we were ramping up for a good New Year celebration at the club. Tickets had sold well, and it was to be a sparkly, lively and exciting evening. Dad was supposed to come a few days after Christmas to stay with us into the New Year, as he had taken to spending Christmas with my brother and his wife in Minneapolis. This was to be the first Christmas for Garry and his wife's new twin girl and boy, born just the January before.

I got a call from Dad before he was to leave for Minneapolis that he wasn't feeling great, and he was thinking of cancelling the trips. I was terribly disappointed and told him still to come, we'd take it slow and take care of him. He relented and when he arrived from Minneapolis the day before New Year's, he seemed exhausted and again much thinner. But he rallied for New Year's and we had a momentous night at the club after a dinner out with friends for Peking duck, the first time Dad and I had ever had it. When I look at the picture our friend took of Dad and I, laughing with his arm around me at the table, I can still feel him close. At the stroke of midnight when we popped open bottles of champagne at the club with Tony's younger brothers there, Dad threw down his cane and did a little jig, giving each of us in turn the biggest bear-hug. It was such a wonderful night.

The next day at our house, Dad had trouble getting out of bed to take his pills, so I brought them to him in bed. He was exhausted from the effort to swallow them all and it was hard for him to come downstairs for supper. We were beyond worried. The next day, when Tony had gone to the club to work on accounts, Dad slowly made his way downstairs and sat with his head down at the kitchen table, clearly having a difficult time breathing. He couldn't summon the energy to take his pills, let alone have tea and breakfast and I told him I was going to call an ambulance.

Waiting, terrified for the ambulance after getting all of Dad's pills together, I called Tony in a panic. He quickly said he'd meet me at Emergency. When we got there, Dad was clearly in pain just trying to breathe. They put him on a stretcher in the hallway in the back, awaiting a room but I begged for someone to give him something to help with the pain. Holding his hand as the waves of pain wracked his body, I felt so helpless to do anything. Tony arrived soon afterwards and was shocked to see Dad's condition. He promised to hold Dad's hand while I told Dad I was going to phone Garry.

Garry was incredulous. He had noticed Dad seemed to tire easily during his visit out there, but was he really that ill? I screamed at him that he was having trouble breathing and even then, it was extremely painful. He told me to call him when we found anything out and I rang off in utter frustration. Returning quickly to Tony at Dad's side, it took 3 hours for them to get him into a bed. They had determined (after a painful chest X-ray), that Dad's lymph nodes (which were now apparently cancerous, as well) were draining into his lungs and they were going to attempt to drain them. It meant puncturing Dad's lungs from behind and they asked us to leave for the procedure. Tony reassured Dad that it would be much better and held me while they did it. When we returned, Dad looked so much better and was breathing easily. His oxygen level, which had been scarily far below normal, had returned to normal. They were going to monitor him and then return him back home to us.

Later that night when we returned home with Dad, he admitted to us that the doctors at home had discovered the cancer had spread to his other kidney and perhaps his liver, but we were all still optimistic that the experimental pill regimen would work. Before discharging Dad, the doctors and nurses warned me that Dad needed a shot in his abdomen twice a day to ensure that he wouldn't get blood clots in his legs. I was terrified at the responsibility, never having given an injection before, but Dad smiled at me and told me he wouldn't even squeak if it hurt, bless him.

After putting Dad to bed, I called Garry and tried to explain to him the seriousness of the situation. Like me, he hadn't known that the cancer had spread. I couldn't believe when he asked me point-blank if I knew that "this was it", was Dad dying? I stared at the phone in disbelief and Tony saw my expression of horror. He quietly took the phone from me and said to Garry that he needed to get up here, there were decisions that may need to be made and I was doing everything. Dad needed us both. At last Garry relented, and Dad looked so happy when we told him the next day that Garry was coming. He held my hand and told me that all he had ever wanted was for his 2 kids to be close and take care of each other when he was gone. Later that day his condition worsened, and he couldn't get out of bed. I called the ambulance again and stayed in Emergency with Dad while Tony went to pick Garry up at the airport.

Throughout this ordeal, Jackie had insisted on coming to the hospital and had Jeff drop her off. David was refusing to come once he found out his Uncle Garry was there, as he felt so hurt and abandoned by Garry not maintaining any contact with them. I pleaded with him to come see his Grandpa, but he said only if his uncle wasn't there.

This time, they didn't send Dad home from Emergency. He was put in the first of 3 hospital wards and Garry and I knew it was of utmost importance to get our Uncle Bill, Dad's younger brother, here from Ireland. We called Uncle Bill from our house later that night, after Dad had been settled in to his hospital room and seemed to be resting somewhat comfortably. At first, Uncle Bill didn't know if he could come, as his health was failing as well and he, himself was on 2 walking-sticks. At 6 feet 6, he had had 3 hip-replacement surgeries and they hadn't gone well. I had always known him as an energetic, fun-loving man who I only met on trips over to England during my childhood or when he visited with Mom and Dad, then Dad after Mom had died.

We had never been allowed to be particularly close to Dad's family. My mother's jealousy at his connection with his own family, so far away caused many a row through the years. Even when we did visit, she would frequently tell Garry and me (without my father or anyone else nearby) that Uncle Bill and his wife Jeanie "hated children" and to stay away from them. Little did I know that they were heartbroken that they couldn't have children, themselves and had adopted a young teenaged girl from difficult circumstances growing up, to help her through school and college. They adored my Aunt's many nieces and nephews and were anything but child-haters! Our relationship had always been from a distance and we had never really gotten close but that was to change…

Uncle Bill arrived the next day, to stay at a hotel nearby us and the hospital. He didn't want to impose with Garry already staying with us, although we would have been thrilled to have him there. The look on my Dad's face when Uncle Bill sauntered in on his canes was priceless. He looked so relieved to have his "big little brother" there, I knew we'd made the right decision. The pain was getting worse and the doctors were having a difficult time controlling it. Garry, Uncle Bill, Jackie and I stayed with Dad around the clock while Tony had to work at the club and his own business and would come after hours, exhausted but supportive and loving towards all of us.

Garry decided that he knew he had to stay but wanted to get a few things in order back at the office and bring his wife and the kids up to see Dad, so he left after a few days to return with them the next day. I offered to have them stay at the house, but Garry's wife wanted her own place…a furnished apartment nearby for her, Garry and the kids. I found one nearby, quite nice, behind the Wal-mart and near both us and the hospital. I picked them up at the airport the next day, so happy to finally meet my adorable niece and nephew.

Dad was thrilled to see the kids and Garry with his wife and seemed to rally a little, but the doctors told us there was no hope anymore…the cancer had spread to his liver. Dad's appetite was waning and I struggled to bring him the foods that he enjoyed, everything from tropical fruits to milk with sugar and raw eggs (my grandmother used to make him that when he was going out to a sporting activity growing up and he loved it), but he was only barely existing on meal supplements and his meals were returned untouched.

Jackie refused to go to school, insisting on being with her beloved Grandpa every waking moment and Jeff (uncharacteristically) relented. Even David came by one morning early (before Garry got there) to spend some time with Dad. He talked to him about his hopes and dreams and Dad managed to talk him out of going into the Music program at university, to work towards a Business Degree and eventually an MBA. He was a smart boy but confused and Dad patiently heard him out, giving him sage and wise advice, for which I will always be indebted to him.

While all this was happening, I was calling Dad's wife Arlene daily to keep her up on his prognosis and condition. She was refusing to come but insisted on talking to Dad over the phone about the bills that were coming through and needed to be paid. His frustration and hurt at her attitude clearly showed how much he was hurt by this, but he never complained. She did relent to come a few weeks later, along with one of her daughters. I picked them up at the airport, to bring them to the hospital but they said they wanted to "check in" at the hotel first. When I offered to wait for them to bring them over, they said they wanted to settle in and would take a taxi over later.

Garry and I were taking a breather by the elevator when they arrived while Jackie and Uncle Bill stayed with Dad. The moment Arlene saw Garry, she brought out some bills she said needed to be paid. He went red and almost exploded, sputtering that "now was not the time" and she flounced off to Dad's room. All of us left to give them some privacy while her daughter sat down in a chair to read passages of the Bible and Arlene twittered around Dad.

When we returned half-an-hour later, Dad was sitting up in bed with his legs over the edge on the phone, weakly trying to dial his telephone banking account to pay the bills Arlene was insisting needed to be paid. She left after that, kissing Dad on the forehead and refused to return before leaving the next day to fly back home to Winnipeg. I think it was at that point that Dad just stopped eating altogether. We did manage to celebrate the twins' first birthday with the cake we brought to the hospital and the many presents Tony and I had bought them to open and play with there. David even got in on spending time with the twins, meeting Garry's wife and me at a kids' play-place for an afternoon while Uncle Bill and Tony stayed with Dad.

I hardly showered, ate, slept or left the hospital for almost 3 weeks. Tony was frantically trying to keep up with his business (which he had reduced considerably) and the club. Dad's condition was worsening, and he was almost unable to leave the bed but insisted on not using the bed-pan. Understanding Dad's need to retain some dignity, Garry and I would help lift him out of bed and drag along the 2 poles and 6 lines into his arms to get him to the washroom. Dad was so weak that he would lean his poor head on Garry's stomach and I'd squeeze his hand, while little came out since so little had gone into him other than medication.

One night, as the 9 of us were in Dad's room, Tony set about to write something on a pad of paper on the floor outside Dad's room. He scratched away at it for several hours and then came in to read to Dad the most beautiful letter you could ever imagine. He proceeded to tell Dad how much he appreciated all of the people around him who loved him so much, going through each of us in turn. He pointed out the wonderful things about each of us and finished with me…getting down on his knee to propose to me right there, in front of everyone. The smile and tears of joy on Dad's face I will never forget. Tony hadn't wanted Dad to miss a thing and he knew that. He and Dad hugged for a long time and everyone was in tears. It was a most special moment to share with them all.

They moved Dad to the Palliative Care ward the next morning and tried to move him out of his bed, which was one of those special ones that uses air to keep every part of the body afloat in areas that need it. I've never seen my Uncle Bill angry, never mind so angry and he yelled at them and shook one of his sticks at them, preventing them from taking his "big brother" out of his comfortable bed. They relented, and Dad stayed as comfortable as he could be, despite the pain. His veins were collapsing, and they had to start to use "butterflies" just under his skin on his chest to administer his medications. I will never forget the kindness of the nurses there, one who Dad took to in particular. He always asked them their names and when he asked her when she'd be back, she sadly looked away and said: "next week". I knew the end was near.

We were all frantic when Dad's medications didn't work anymore. I had called the Cancer Clinic, but they were unable to get him in until much later and the hospital called the Pain Clinic to see what else they could give him. We were always running up to the desk begging them to give Dad something else, something more, as he would writhe in pain with no respite. We were helpless to do anything and one day when he was more lucid, Dad asked Garry and I to talk to the doctor, to have him "give him too much" of something to take him out of his misery. Although I didn't want to, I did dutifully ask and the doctor explained that he just couldn't do it.

The one morning that both Garry and I had gone back home to take a quick shower, I called on my way back as I drove into the hospital parking lot. It was the only time since Dad had been in hospital that we were both away at the same time. Jackie answered in tears, Grandpa had just died. I ran as fast as I could after parking, calling Tony and Garry on the way.

When I got there, Uncle Bill was standing by Dad, with all the machines turned off. Jackie had been amazing, he assured me, as she saw Dad struggling and stood right by him as the nurses and doctors worked on him, holding his hand and telling him it was okay,

"Grandma is waiting for you".

Jackie was beside herself and sobbed in my arms as I came in. Uncle Bill calmly said that his big brother wasn't in pain anymore. Tony had called David, and Garry arrived as Tony walked in. We both held Dad's hands, those incredibly big, strong but loving, gentle hands. I whispered to him that I loved him forever and to give Mom our love. David arrived a few moments later and walked into the room stony-faced. He refused to go near Dad and looked in from the doorway, running out to a friend's running car and leaving. I called him, and he said he "just couldn't handle it", he had to go.

We stayed in the room for a while. The nurses had removed Dad's wedding ring from his hand. Garry picked it up with shaking hands and we marvelled at how big Dad's hands had been. It was bigger than even any of our thumbs. The realization that those huge yet gentle hands would never hold us again was more than I could bear. I called Arlene from the hallway. She responded without emotion and asked us to call her with whatever arrangements that needed to be made.

That night, Uncle Bill suggested that we all go out for a dinner to celebrate Dad's life, as he wanted to treat us all. It was a lively but sombre evening as we shared stories about our beloved father, brother and grandfather. That night, Garry and I tried to figure out how to bring Dad's body back to Winnipeg for the funeral. We wanted him to come by train, as he had worked for the railway until his retirement, but the railway couldn't figure out how to do it. So, we flew him and Garry, his wife and the kids, Jackie, Uncle Bill and I flew along. We stayed in the hotel that Mom and Dad had had their wedding reception in so many years before. David had refused to come.

There was so much to do. Jackie helped Garry's wife look after the kids while he and I raced around to Dad's lawyers, accountants and business managers. We had to find the Will, which wasn't in his safety deposit box, where we thought it would be. Arlene was being incredibly obstructive and wouldn't let us into the house (actually technically owned by us now, as it was in Dad's name) to get the keys in the first place. His lawyer didn't think he had it and we were left to hopefully find it in the house. She said she'd let us in later the next day (with her daughter and her daughter's girlfriend and her daughter's ex-girlfriend and her ex-girl-friend's girl-friend there) and Uncle Bill resolved to get involved at this point. He saw where this was going.

First, we went to Dad's car (in the garage, the battery had run dry, so we had a difficult time opening the trunk), where we knew he often kept important papers in his briefcase that he hadn't brought with him. While trying to open the trunk, we noticed smaller finger-prints on the top of the trunk that looked like a woman's. Arlene stood smugly by as we opened the trunk to find nothing.

When Garry and I came inside, the daughter asked us where we were going and when he saw the flash of anger in my eyes, Uncle Bill took over to entertain them all. "None of your business, to our father's room," I countered. Dad and Arlene had had separate bedrooms and now I knew why. Garry and I looked everywhere. A knock at the door was the daughter again, how long would we be? "As long as it takes," I snarled. Garry and I were at our wits-end. Dad's computer had nothing on it of importance and none of his paper files in his desk were relevant, but I pulled out the file drawer and found taped behind it a file. It was the Will. Dad had seemed to know that Arlene was a piranha but was unable to drive to his lawyer's or safety deposit box. I guess he knew that the end was near…he had drafted a new Will that the lawyers had a copy of, but not the original. Arlene saw us coming out with the file and acted flustered and too sweet. We left grimly, imagining Dad's life with this wretched woman.

The next day, Garry and I met with the pastor of the church where Dad had asked me to have his service. Of course, Arlene was there, it being her church. I explained to the man, who Dad used to get together with for beers and ribs to watch hockey and football games with, what had been Dad's wishes. Dad was not a religious man, but he was a spiritual person. I told him that we wanted (at Dad's request) to not have a very religious ceremony, with no gospel music, accompanied by his favourite (tasteful) jazz classics. Arlene sweetly asked me how long I'd been away from Winnipeg, how well did I know my father. I thought Garry was going to lose it…"Very well, we talked on the phone almost every day", I shot back.

Seeing the interchange, the pastor looked uncomfortable. I pressed upon him the friendship that he had had with Dad, that as a friend, he had wanted him to do the service. He explained that they had another pastor (female) that did services with him and I replied that wasn't our father's wishes, but he insisted.

Arlene pouted and asked if she could have one hymn played that was her favorite…we relented, of course. I finished by saying that we would have an open-casket and she looked shocked. I challenged her that that was how our family did it and he was a handsome man, wasn't he? I asked that we be put behind a screen of drapes at the front, as we don't care to show our grief publicly, welcoming her to join us with the rest of the family. She replied that she wanted to be out with her "congregation of friends" up front and I was relieved to not have her with us. That being done, Garry and I picked up his wife, the kids and Jackie to go to the funeral parlour for a meeting.

When we got the parlour, which is the same one that had buried everyone in my family, the "consultant" explained to us that in unearthing my parents' dual urn, they had broken it trying to open it and it wouldn't hold 2 people's ashes, anyway. I was outraged and disgusted. Garry looked about to lose it. I calmly explained that when I had helped my father choose the urn for our mother (the most expensive one there, Dad had chosen one with a young couple sitting on a park-bench, a bird on the back of the bench behind them), he had been assured that it was for a couple.

The fellow said that he had nothing to do with things done over 10 years before and I told him that they had sold my father something extremely expensive, in his time of greatest agony, that was a lie. He began to look uncomfortable and starter to sputter. "What would you like me to do, the other one is broken, anyways?" He nervously tried to smooth things over. "I think you should show us what you have that holds 2 and give it to us at below cost price, for misleading my father," I retorted. "But I can't, I have to talk to my manager," he blubbered. "You just do that, you're like a used-car salesman," I said, unable to contain myself.

The guy returned, nodding that it was okay and we stood up to look at what they had in stock. Jackie, Garry, his wife and I looked through their inventory and found a simple but beautiful one. Having chosen it, I told the guy to show us their paperwork on it. Seeing their cost-price, I told him to make it 10% less for the trouble they had put us through. He looked down and relented, then quickly asked for a credit card to begin the process. I replied that everything was to be paid for through my Dad's estate, to bill it to them, although Garry had quickly pulled out his credit card. I told him to put it back. The guy said he needed to see his manager (again) and returned, saying it was "irregular", but would be fine.

When we left the place, Garry broke down in tears of anger and frustration. He couldn't believe what they had put us through. I was just plain mad. Although feeling beyond devastated myself, I reminded him that Dad had trusted us with his wishes and our parents had raised us to fight for what we thought was right.

Uncle Bill, Tony, Garry and I had scoured the web for the jazz tunes that Dad had loved and found his favourites to compile a CD for the service. So many of them we could picture Dad in our minds, lying back and listening to them in his favorite chair and dancing tenderly with Mom to the ballads. Whatever anyone thought, we resolved, Dad would be celebrated his own way in his own style.

The day of the funeral, I got there early with Uncle Bill and Jackie, hoping to find the minister before the service began. I wanted to ensure that he would follow our (and Dad's) wishes about the tone of the service. He reassured me that he would do his best for his friend and we seated ourselves behind the screened curtain. Arlene was seated up-front, dabbing at her eyes in front of Dad's casket with many of her cronies around her. The music began playing…a musical hymn of some sort that just seemed to keep on going. Arlene looked victorious, as it turned out the song was one of her friends' compositions and this was the first "public" presentation. Enraged, I went over to the "consultant" and told him to change it from the 13-minute droning music. He looked flustered but acquiesced, just in time for the minister to begin his sermon. Thankfully, he had kept his word and talked about the mysteries of the universe, the "great circle of life" and Dad's place in it…no religious allusions, no prophets, no lessons or parables. Similarly, his female partner (who seemed so out-of-place and pointless) followed the theme.

After the service, which followed to the strains of Dad's favourite jazz as people filed out to the reception upstairs, with the room emptied we all emerged from behind the curtains to see Dad for the last time. As we all stared at Dad's handsome, peaceful face for the last time, Garry hugged his wife and Jackie clung to them. I sobbed like my heart was breaking on my own and dear Uncle Bill came out from behind the curtains to envelope me. He had said that he hadn't wanted to see Dad in the casket, preferring to remember him as he was in life, but he couldn't stand seeing me look so forlorn, abandoned and alone. Tony hadn't been able to make it because of the businesses or he would have been out there with me. Uncle Bill's selfless act to stand by me and hold me in my time of need is something I will never forget.

Once we had composed ourselves, we entered the reception room, and were surrounded with Dad's colleagues and their families. Aging gentlemen and ladies themselves, they were crestfallen to lose their mentor, their boss, co-worker and friend. Many of them had seen Garry and I grow up, meeting us at company kid Christmas parties through the years. There were so many of them and if I hadn't realized it before, Dad was as beloved and respected a man in his business world as he was in ours.

Arlene was flouncing around with her church-ladies, studiously avoiding us and occasionally dabbing her eyes with a Kleenex when she saw people looking at her. But I saw no sadness in those eyes, just a sharp appraisal of all those around her. The minister approached me for the cheque, which I proffered to him…for the services of himself alone, not his "associate", who was busy scoffing down as much of the sandwiches and pastries as she could seem to hold. It may have been (and probably was) a petty gesture on my part, but as far as I was concerned, her services were redundant and neither requested nor required.

As the crowd started to thin out and only Arlene and her ladies-in-waiting remained along with us, she minced over to us and asked sweetly if she could bundle up the remaining goodies to take home with her. "Help yourself, we don't want any of it," I replied. She just had to get her last free meal off of Dad. Sickened, we left the building, drained and empty. There would be no funeral cortege to bury Dad with Mom in their urn together at this time, because the perma-frost prevented it (Winnipeg weather in January). Garry and I had resolved to bury them on their wedding anniversary, in May later in the Spring.

Uncle Bill flew back home to Ireland from Winnipeg, he, Garry and I having resolved to keep in close contact. Dad had asked Uncle Bill to please keep us all together, to look out for each other and being a man of his word, he phoned Garry and I every week to maintain the connection. His wisdom, compassion and patience, having him back in my life made such a difference and I am so thankful to Dad for that. Profound loss sometimes brings new beginnings...

Chapter 15: Feeling Lost, Then Found

It seems strange for someone to hear that one can feel like an orphan as an older adult, but that was how I felt...the cushion of the older generation was no longer there, and I was "up to bat". I missed Dad terribly and can't even begin to enumerate how many times I'd reach for the phone to ask him or tell him something, then remember he wasn't there anymore. Tony, too was missing Dad greatly. They had become very close and he had come to see Dad as a mentor, a father-figure who believed in him unconditionally.

Getting back into work-mode was tough, but I had to do it. David would sometimes call me to get together for lunch and I saw the emptiness in his eyes as he talked about Dad. He asked about the wedding, when were Tony and I going to get married? I answered that we had planned for June 4th, which would have been Dad's 75th birthday. But I knew nothing could happen until the divorce was complete and resolved to make it happen.

I started pushing Bob, my lawyer, again to move things forward. No, I wasn't going to go to court and argue about the large amount of money that Jeff had taken from me. I wanted it done, with whatever there was left to declare divided fairly. The marital house had sold finally (although way under what it was worth, thanks to our useless real estate agent), and Jeff and the kids had moved into his new house. Jackie still came over on her weeks with us and I would take

David out on lunches whenever he agreed to come, but he never came back to live with us again.

At the end of my rope and with time ticking by to get the divorce decree done in time for a wedding, I emailed Jeff that I wanted to get things done, could he just get his lawyer to get back to mine. He curtly replied that she wasn't getting back to him, either and none of it was his fault. I left a message at his lawyer's office that I was coming over to meet with her, and miraculously she sent a letter replying to Bob's last…we were going to "strike a deal", but it was too late to have the wedding in June by this time. Uncle Bill and Aunt Jeanie had already booked their flights to come over for the wedding and we were paralyzed to do anything about it, so decided to have an engagement party at the club instead.

The deal that Jeff presented was splitting everything he declared (which wasn't much, just what remained from the sale of the marital house) down the middle. Because I couldn't stand to see his face anymore, I emailed him back that I deserved my share of the motorcycles and their trailer he had sold (he said for very little), the boat (which he said the guy never paid him for?!), and the money from my grandparents' will ($15,000) and my $30,000 contribution that bought us our first home. None of the money for that home had come from Jeff. He reluctantly agreed, and it was over…a lifetime of work, scrimping and saving left me with $120,000. The forensic accountant I had hired before had estimated that there was almost a million dollars that had disappeared somewhere. It was pathetic, but at least it was done. I had danced my last dance with the devil.

Aunt Jeanie and Uncle Bill arrived a few days before the party and we had a marvellous time with them. They had booked to stay for 5 weeks and we had great plans to take them all around the province. They were thrilled to be with us and we forged a wonderful, close bond. The kids adored them and couldn't wait to spend as much time with them as possible. Our party was a wonderful time with Tony's huge family of siblings, aunts, uncles and cousins, my little family and so many friends who turned up. Our staff worked hard to make it a success and joined in the festivities. Dad would have been thrilled, we thought...

The wedding was another matter. The final divorce decree came through well into the late summer, after Uncle Bill and Aunt Jeanie had returned home to Ireland. We knew it would be hard for them financially to come back for the wedding, but they so wanted to share in the joy with us, so Tony and I told them we'd pay for their accommodations if they could cover the flight, which they were thrilled to agree to. It just wouldn't have been our special day without them.

Jackie agreed to sing us down the aisle to Natalie Cole's "When I Fall in Love" and David was even getting into the excitement of it all. We planned for a September wedding on a date Tony's mother had chosen as "lucky". Tony and I had to decide where the ceremony should take place. He agreed (thankfully) with me that I couldn't get married in a Catholic church, as I wasn't about to convert but he really wanted to be able to complete the sacrament with a Holy Communion. I had been baptized in the Anglican

Church as an infant and suggested we look into their practices. Sure enough, Communion was part of their services and Tony agreed to have our wedding at the local Anglican Church. The minister was a lovely man, who saw my discomfort at trying to explain I was divorced at our first meeting. He quickly told us that he, too, had been divorced from his wife of many years but had found love again with his new wife. That made a huge difference to me, as he understood where I was coming from. We still had to take the marriage classes along with the other couples marrying in the church and found them interesting, generating lots of discussions.

Tony's mother wasn't thrilled with the wedding not being in a Roman Catholic Church, but she still happily threw herself into helping us with preparations. As Tony had so many friends, he chose 12 attendants. I could only think of 6 (including Jackie and Alixe, of course), and we set about to choose how to stage it. We had invited my Aunt from Winnipeg and I was even willing to drive there and get her, but she felt that she couldn't leave Uncle, even for a couple of days. She still maintains that we never invited her...

We never did get invitations out in the mail to people, but simply emailed and/or phoned people 2 weeks before the wedding date. In retrospect, it was beyond ridiculously rushed, but we would make it work. Some of Tony's relatives from Italy were going to be able to make it, others couldn't because of the short notice but all who lived here in Canada, spread out from coast-to-coast were coming. Not being a "young bride" and not feeling it was appropriate to wear white, I decided to have my "girls" wear black. I had heard stories of women stuck with gaudy-coloured dresses from weddings they had been a part of years before and resolved to have each choose a dress that fit her style and body-type, so that she could wear it again.

When Aunt Jeanie and Uncle Bill arrived, we took Jackie out to find her a lovely dress and then the 4 of us went dress-shopping for me. I found a lovely mid-length, low-cut black cocktail dress that they all said was "perfect!" and our shopping trip was a success.

Tony and I had asked my brother Garry and his wife to be in the wedding party and they had been thrilled. Tony wanted Garry, a terrific speaker, to be the master-of-ceremonies. A week before the wedding, they cancelled on us, saying that their recent move made it too difficult for them to come. But Tony's best friend, who had just moved down to Texas with his growing family, was thrilled to take on the role. Thank heavens for his kindness.

One of my brides-maid's friends was a florist and her gift to me was the flowers. I had chosen white gladioli and blue roses...the blue from the colours we had chosen for our nightclub. Food for the reception, which we were doing as a buffet was provided as a gift from one of our business associates. The liquor came from our own store-house at the club. David was thrilled to get measured up for his tuxedo rental with Tony and the two forged a close bond from that experience together. Tony had booked a "party bus" to take us girls to the church and then the wedding party to a lovely park for pictures after the ceremony amidst its beautiful gardens. One of my brides-maid's fathers was a photographer and he was taking our pictures.

So, the night before the wedding, I packed myself up and went to Alixe's for a sleepover and to get ready together the next morning. We woke up early the next morning and raced to the hair-dresser's she knew. I asked for a simpler style, not too fancy but with some baby's breath entwined in my hair. With lots of hairspray and a few dangling curls that later came down, I started to panic as she began on Alixe's long, thick hair. Time was getting short and we still had to get back to her house, get changed and meet the party-bus to drive us to the church. Well, we didn't make the bus, they left without us. I raced us across town in my car, making it 1 minute before the ceremony was to begin. Tony said that the car sprayed showers of sparks as I sped over the speed-bumps into the church parking-lot, but I made it! He had been standing outside, looking a little green-around the gills.

When we got inside, Tony's brothers told us that he had been shaky and pale, almost keeling over…was it fear or second-thoughts or anxiety? I didn't know, but as we lined up to the strains of Jackie's heavenly voice resounding a cappella throughout the church, Tony pulled me close and held my hand tightly as we walked up the aisle. It was a memorable ceremony with so many friends, business associates and so much family sharing in our joy.

Tony and I had written our own vows and after I had recited mine, he shakily took his out. It took him a few seconds to get the words out, he was so choked up and with tears in his eyes, his voice was shaking. I reached out to hold his hand and that seemed to steady him, so he went on. There were murmurs in the audience, as they saw that gesture, of reaching out to help the other, the very characteristic that was the epitome of us as a couple. Our ages, our stages of life, our religions, our cultures, our history didn't matter…what made us work was that we somehow inexplicably fit, understood each other so well and filled each other's needs without even having to say anything.

Full of surprises, Tony's cousin from Vancouver turned on one of my favourite Kiss tunes over the speaker system as we walked back up the aisle at the end of the service. I don't think that kind of music had ever been played in a church before, but the minister was a very understanding and kind man. We got on the party-bus and headed for the park.

The pictures turned out beautifully and we had such fun having them taken. When we arrived at the club for the reception, we were a little worried to find my Aunt and Uncle not there yet. When they didn't answer the phone at their hotel (they had returned to their room after the ceremony to have a rest), we were even more worried. One of our friends, a retired police officer, was about to call in some favors from old colleagues to be on the lookout for an elderly couple between their hotel and the club when they arrived, refreshed and dressed for a night-on-the-town. Tony's brother Todd had made a wonderful slide show of both of us growing up (Tony had gotten him into my childhood photo albums) and it was hilarious to see mine in black-and-white, styles from the 60's and 70's, and his from the 70's and 80's. What a treasure it was and incredibly thoughtful for him to have compiled for us!

We didn't have assigned tables, wanting everything to be casual and relaxed but it turned out great. People just sat or stood where they wanted to and mingled so comfortably. Tony's mother and older sisters had decorated the club late the night before and early that morning (I had no idea) and it was beautiful with flowers and decorations. The music was perfect, and Tony and I danced to that first jazz tune he had remembered from that first night we met. Jackie sang another song for us as her wedding present and everyone was so amazed by the maturity of her beautiful, clear voice. Life was good.

Tony, Jackie and I arrived home after the reception and opened a bottle of champagne to toast together. As she sipped her champagne appreciatively, Jackie thoughtfully looked at Tony and declared: "Can I call you Dad, Tony? You've been more of a father to me than Jeff has…" and we almost dropped our glasses. Tony reached out to embrace her with tears in his eyes, quietly replying "I'd be honored, Jackie, but remember that Jeff is and will always be your dad. I can never replace him, nor will I try to, but you have made me a happy man." Our strange little family was continuing to morph in mysterious ways…

Chapter 16: Life in a Nutshell

We never know how things will turn out. Losses turn into finding something new, sometimes even better. You can be looking so hard for something and never find it, then when you least expect it and weren't looking for it, there it is. Like everyone, I had had many losses in my life, but I just think they were there to make me dig deeper and grow stronger. Sometimes it doesn't turn out that way and it's all give-and-take. But it's how we live it, how we turn things around towards the future that makes all the difference. Our past contributes to who we become, but it's what we do with it that makes us who we are.

I never knew how things would turn out and of course life is ongoing. The turmoil of my childhood had made me a strong, independent woman but I had gone-with-the-flow, styling myself more as a wife and mother once the kids were born. Maybe it was the guilt at having to go back to work earlier than I had wanted after the kids' births, but I had to because every time we seemed to settle down, Jeff had somehow lost his job. As my father had said, at least we created two wonderful kids together. Maybe that was the overall purpose of our union. It certainly wasn't to make me a happier person, that's for sure. Maybe we can only learn and grow through pain, devastation and renewal. Or maybe it's just me...I could never seem to give up on anything, instead struggling to finish everything I have begun, no matter what it took.

I have (like many) endured abuse from people in my life and seemed to keep on taking it, as if I deserved it. Staying home for so long to help nurture Garry as long as I could, my mother's recriminations and bitterness left me unsure of myself in almost every area of my life except in my education and subsequent career. I had met Jeff at a vulnerable time away from home for the first time and he was an anchor, a place to belong. Sometimes relationships are only supposed to be for a time, but it carried into my future and despite the frequent moves and having to start over again and again, I learned a lot about my business and myself along the way.

My kids had become the driving force behind everything I did, once they were born. Their every breath, every desire, hope and dream became mine. I found myself in motherhood but lost who I was in the process. Maybe it was that overwhelming passion to be the best mother I could be that drove the wedge between Jeff and me. I'll never know, but I do know that I gave him everything I had to give, and he took it, giving nothing in return.

You'd think I'd be bitter and unable to trust again, but somehow Tony made it so easy to love him. I never once questioned his intentions, despite all the warnings from my friends. I was still that wide-eyed girl who had given him the key to my town-house and then my heart. He helped give me my confidence back as a business-woman, as a professional, as a mother and as a partner in life. He had won my family's hearts, trust and love, from my beloved Dad to my brother Garry to my loving Aunt Jeanie and Uncle Bill. Even with everything we went through with the kids, they couldn't help but love and respect him.

Of course, I am saddened by what the end of my marriage did to the kids, but I tried to play it fair, just as I did the divorce. Good guys don't always finish first and it was never a competition for me, but we can't control or know how the other players are going to play. The kids were hurt and became pawns as I struggled to continue on, being the same parent I had always been. I just wasn't willing to compromise my relationship with them to become their friend, which unfortunately sometimes happens. I can only hope that they see the truth as they become adults and grow into their own relationships.

What I do know is that I grew from pain and losses. Losing my mother made Dad and me closer. Losing Dad brought Uncle Bill and Aunt Jeanie closer. Losing Jeff made me open to meeting the person who is the closest I have ever felt to anyone. Knowing my agony at the struggles with the kids, Uncle Bill has always reminded me that at the end of the day, kids grow and move on with their lives but who we have in our lives is who has chosen to be there.

Would I have ever in my wildest dreams seen myself happily remarried to a man so different from me, yet so much the perfect complement to me? No, I never had time for dreams or imagining anything other than the struggles of life as I knew it. Now I have someone to dream with, to share hopes and plans for the future with, to lean on and be leaned on, to laugh and cry with, to love and be loved unconditionally. I have rebuilt and found myself again, learned not to be so self-critical, not to be overcome by guilt, to trust myself again. I have hope when before there was no hope. Life goes on and that is mine…in a nutshell.

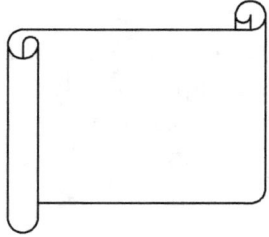